k—,

You are one of my

truest inspirations!

Thank you for all you

do, for me and for RAW!

Moment of Truth

Mark Watters

8-19-06

Moment of Truth

Mark R. Watters

Moment of Truth

Mark R. Watters

www.lulu.com/MarkWatters/

For **Christina** and **Kristyn**.

Moment of Truth

Mark R. Watters

Dead Rebels in Hog Trough Road (Bloody Lane), September 19, 1862
Alexander Gardner

Moment of Truth

"Now the wind is still,
In a moment it will be raging;
Now my soul is young,
In a moment it will be aging."

-- Dan Fogelberg

Moment of Truth

Mark R. Watters

Hog Trough Road (Bloody Lane), April 2004

Moment of Truth

Moment of Truth

Moment of Truth

Chapter 1

The September breeze pushed the fertile foliage like a rolling sea of emerald and gold, corn and wheat swishing the sweet air. It was an idyll, a tease, set against the ominous backdrop of a nation at war with itself, gray clouds stalking a blue sky. It was a township squeezed between devils and gods gripped in an epochal struggle to define a nation's future or ratify its past. It was a time of contrast, predictable and fickle, tranquil and explosive. It was a haven of plenty for hungry soldiers and a fine spot for the business of war.

The valley of the Antietam drifted through its moments of routine turbulence, like a butterfly in a spring zephyr. Late summer thunder marched across the horizon, a crescendo of alternating piano and forte. A storm lurked like none other.

Devil's darning needles, clinging one atop the other in docile domination, zipped around Jacob and Rachael.

"Watch out, Rachael!" Jacob yelled, teasing. "They'll *suck* your brains out *through your ears!*"

"That's just silly!" Rachael said, squealing, dodging the six-legged projectiles. "Where'd you hear a thing like that? Dragonflies are as gentle as butterflies, only ugly."

"Keep talking, Jasmine! Else them things'll sew your lips together!" Jacob insisted.

Moment of Truth

Hand over her mouth, Rachael evaded the unpredictable paths of the insects, ducking her head, swinging her hips, and using Jacob as her shield.

"The one on top's the Yankee!" she said through her fingers. "He's gawn ride that Reb like a wild mare, then suck *his* brains out!"

"Rachael, what are you *talkin'* about?" Jacob asked.

"Oh, a little of *this*, a little of *that*, a little of why-don't-you-come-over-here," she sang.

"What kind of talk is that on a Sunday afternoon anyhow?"

Rachael blew seeds off a dandelion. "Just talk. Anyway, I hear tell Roswell's joinin' up with Lee," she said, head tilted one way and eyes the other. A bouquet of blue phlox and Black-Eyed Susans wilted in her hand.

"Ain't no such a thing!" Jacob said, yanking up some clover and picking through the bunch for four-leafers. "Ros is just fifteen, like me, and besides, his Daddy would skin him six ways from Sunday."

"Ain't what I hear," Rachael said, hands on hips. "Roswell says he's doin' it, maybe today. Said he's been spendin' time over at Pack Horse Ford, just sittin' and watchin' the river like it was callin' his name or somethin'."

"It's all because you dared him, Rachael, just like you done me! Ros has always liked you, an' he'll do just about anything to impress a perty girl."

Rachael smiled, handing Jacob her bouquet. "I like a man in uniform. You'd be right cute yourself–without the flowers."

Jacob blushed. "The only uniform I ever seen on a reb is a suit of rags. Look, Rachael, just because the rebs licked Pope at Manassas don't mean the war's over. They're out-gunned, out-manned, out-supplied–"

"But they ain't out-*spirited*," she countered.

BAM!

16

Jacob's bouquet burst into yellow and blue powder as he jerked back his hand in reaction to the explosion.

"What in the *hell*–"

"Roswell!" shouted Rachael, eyes beaming.

"Damn, Ros, you tryin' to *kill* me?"

"If I was tryin' to kill you, you'd be dead now," Roswell answered, walking toward the pair, a smoking musket and a rebel flag in tow. "I couldn't resist such a *yellow* target."

Rachael giggled.

"An' why are you haulin' that ol' reb flag around with you like some child's blanket?" Jacob asked. "Folks around here would string you up for less."

"Well?" nudged Roswell.

"Well *what?*" Jacob replied, brushing pieces of Black-Eyed Susans from his shirt and face.

"I'm leavin' this evenin', after supper."

"To join Lee?" Jacob asked.

"To join Lee. Got my rifle cleaned an' ready. You comin'?"

Jacob fidgeted, brushing off more flower debris. "I don't reckon my Daddy … I spect I ought not, what with the corn needin' harvestin' an' such."

"You ain't got that much corn to harvest, Jacob. Ain't Bigun an' his family takin' care of that?"

"Well, yeah, but there's the wagon business an' all, and–"

"He ain't goin', Roswell," teased Rachael. "Isaac won't *let* 'im."

"My Daddy ain't got *nothin'* to do with this!" Jacob insisted. "There's the corn, and deliverin' wagons to the Furnace, an' who knows what else. The time just ain't right. Maybe in '63."

"By then it'll all be over, and you'll have missed it. I never understood your old man, Jacob," Roswell observed, rubbing invisible dirt off his musket barrel with a tattered rag. "Here he is, a slave-owner, yet he waves Ol' Glory like a trophy. I reckon he's a bit confused. Like you, maybe?"

"Keep my Daddy outa this, Ros, or I'll bust that musket across your skull! The only thing I'm confused about is your eagerness to go an' get yourself killed, an' for *what?* A cause that's as slippery as Hog Trough Road in a spring rain."

"Boys, boys!" feigned Rachael, her desire for a tussle rising. "Let's be … civil."

"Civil, my pimply ass!" Jacob mumbled.

"Jacob, you've always wanted a new rifle," Roswell said, holding up his sparkling Springfield.

"Where'd you get that, anyhow?" Jacob asked.

"Around," Roswell answered, implying connections. "Come on with me and I bet them rebs'll have one for you, straight from Harpers Ferry."

"I ain't fightin' for a country that keeps folks in bondage," Jacob said, arms folded and flowers dangled.

"I ain't either, Jacob. It ain't about bondage itself," argued Roswell. "It's more about states decidin' their own way, without the national government buttin' in."

"But what one state does affects another," Jacob replied, parroting something he had heard pickle-barrel pundits say. "What are there, thirty-five states? Cain't have each one goin' its separate way. They'd be bumpin' into each other left an' right."

"I guess that's why they're fightin' this war. Awful lot of bumpin' goin' on right now. It's a dang mess," Roswell said, his voice fading to a whisper as he looked across the breeze-swept field.

"Anyway, since when did you give a wit about bondage?" Roswell countered. "Bondage is what keeps your Daddy's wagon business a goin' concern. Bondage is all them people knows. Give 'em a little freedom and see how far they get. They *need* the Confederacy. The Union would let 'em go wanderin' around like sick puppies, beggars and thieves, to die on city streets and country paths.

"Your Daddy's just foolin' himself, wavin' them stars and stripes while flauntin' his slaves. South wins, he's a traitor, an' Bigun gets sent to Mississippi to pick cotton. North wins, Bigun goes free. Dang mess."

"Ros, if you were holdin' a wolf by the snout, would you keep holdin' it or let it go?" Jacob asked.

Roswell sidestepped the trap. "I wouldn't be holdin' that wolf in the first place, but some believe they oughta have the right. When Lee whips the Yankees–and he *will*–he'll take Bigun down to the plantations of Mississippi or even Charleston," Roswell said, "and scatter Bigun's family to God-knows-where, an' leave your Daddy with *nothin'*. Maryland's a border state now, but you wait an' see. She'll come around soon enough, I reckon. You, too."

"Aw, you're just flappin' your jaws, Ros," Jacob replied. "Slavery's plain wrong, and you *know* it. Even Rachael knows it! It oughta be the *people*, *all* the people, decidin' their own course, not the wealthy politicians. Besides, you ain't gawn join no rebel army. Come on, Rachael."

Rachael sauntered, hands clasped behind her back, pretending disinterest.

"Go on an' pick your wildflowers, Jacob," Roswell shouted. "We'll see who comes out smellin' like a rose!"

"I'd rather *pick* flowers than *push* 'em outa the ground, Ros. You still comin' to supper tonight?"

Rachael turned back and gave Roswell a coy wave and a wink. She wanted nothing more than to see Roswell tangle with Isaac Hoffman at his own supper table. She believed Roswell had a notch up on Jacob in the "cutes", she called it. No better fun, she figured, than to watch Roswell's sapphire almond eyes penetrate the ire of Jacob's

Daddy. Still, Jacob's vulnerability fed her lust for attention and her eagerness to manipulate. Roswell remained Rachael's 'plan B', for now.

"I'll be there. Seven o'clock?"

"Seven o'clock. Jesse's whippin' up some potpie."

"Chicken?"

"What else? And watch where you're shootin' that dang thing! Somebody's liable to mistake you for the enemy, somebody who ain't holdin' no flowers!"

"Shaw!" Roswell said, dismissing the possibility. "See you at seven."

"Make it six-thirty. Got some cats' eyes if you wanna go a round or two before supper."

Roswell waved and draped the banner around his shoulders and back, and, a song of Dixie on his lips, set off for Pack Horse Ford.

"Somebody's gawn up an' shoot that damn fool!" Jacob said. "Look at 'im. He looks like some *barn door* walkin' across that field."

"I think he's right cute, Jacob Hoffman," Rachael said, admiring Roswell's gait. "You'd be, too, with a flag wrapped around *your* bottom. Even holdin' a bouquet of flowers."

Jacob threw down the shattered remnant of Susans. Rachael giggled.

"Yeah, well, you think a slop hog's cute. Come on. I got to get on home."

Rachael snatched up a sunflower and slapped Jacob's back.

"Ow! Careful, Jasmine! That ain't no flower. That's a dang *dinner plate!*"

Both laughed as they flung flowers and pebbles and stumbled through the fields toward Landing Road and Jacob's home.

Roswell topped a bluff overlooking Pack Horse Ford. The mighty Potomac River bent through the panorama like a sunning snake.

Ten days earlier, Roswell had watched another Roswell, Confederate General Roswell Ripley lead his four brigades in a spirited splash across the Potomac at the Point of Rocks. Men in gray and butternut sang "Maryland, My Maryland" as they negotiated the shallow, swirling waters. Shouts and laughter filled the air, as if these men knew something the rest of the country did not.

Roswell again witnessed the gathering gray bands in Frederick three days later while on a day trip with his daddy. He wanted to join the Rebel army then and there, and would have, had his daddy not seen him cavorting with rebel soldiers near Rosenstock's Dry Goods and Clothing and yanked him away to lunch.

The groups of rebels laughed upon seeing Roswell tugged by the collar. As his daddy pulled him into a restaurant, one rebel hollered, "Come take up a rifle when ya can shave!" Those words rang in Roswell's ears like the bongs of a grandfather clock.

Roswell knew Confederates patrolled the west bank of the Potomac, near Shepherdstown. He was anxious to prove his mettle by wading the river and returning the Rebel battle flag he and Jacob had found a week ago on the Harpers Ferry Road near the Antietam Iron Furnace. He sat and stared at the water's swirls and contemplated the feat, as he had sat he stared day after day.

I'll show them rebs I'm as good as they are! He thought. *I'll bring 'em this flag, holdin' my rifle high, an' I'll do it in front of Yankee eyes.*

He rose from his perch and descended the hillside toward the slapping waters.

Halfway across the knee-deep shallows, Roswell heard the echo of a shout garbled by distance and space.

He stopped and turned, then shrugged and continued. Again the shout came. He ignored it.

Shloop! Shlurp!

Roswell heard the sound, like stones thrown into water. Echoed reports of rifle fire followed. Roswell turned and saw three Yankee soldiers standing at the crest of a hill above the river. As the soldiers reloaded, they yelled something distorted by the breeze and the ripple of water over rocks. The soldiers leveled their rifles. Roswell saw three puffs of dusty white smoke.

Shlurp! Shlurp! Shloop!

Three more shots sliced through the water, this time much closer, close enough to sprinkle his face. Roswell believed the distance too far and his movement too swift to pose any real danger of being hit.

He raised high with one brazened hand a corner of the flag, enough to reveal its blue cross and white stars. He flaunted his rifle in the other hand, as if he possessed a daunting superiority of firepower. He shouted a few obscenities and flashed the finger. His momentary stillness was all the soldiers needed.

Jacob and Rachael arrived home, arm in arm, to the smell of chicken potpie, tomato soup and cornbread, all specialties of Jesse's.

"Git on in here, Missuh Jacob, Miss Rachael! Wash on up and find yo' places," Jesse instructed, a scold in her tone for their childish indiscretion.

Jacob stopped and cupped an ear. "Did you hear that?"

"Yeah, I heard her. Scruffy as ever, she is, but she's a sweetheart," answered Rachael.

"No, not Jesse. Listen. That. That, right there. Hear it?"

"Sounded like cannon fire, toward the mountain."

"It's been buildin', Rachael. Somethin's about to blow."

Rachael looked at Jacob. She thought about Roswell.

Chapter 2

"I got bad news, Jacob," Isaac Hoffman said, his voice competing with the squeaks from a homemade porch rocker.

"Bad news?" Jacob asked through a hollow grin. "Me, too. Supper's cold."

"Hear me out, son. That's why I'm late for supper."

"It's okay, Daddy. Ros is late, too."

"Son, I've been talking to the Chief Burgess. This concerns you."

Jacob looked out across the dusk-draped fields as he yanked cornhusks and silk off cobs. Rachael flicked her paintbrush across the half-finished horizon on her canvass, waiting to see what might emerge.

"What news could possibly be bad on a day like this?" He pulled the collar of his shirt to his forehead and soaked up the sweat. "Except for Ros spoutin' off about joinin' the rebs, today's been …." Jacob stopped. "It's Roswell, ain't it?"

"It's Roswell, son. He's been shot."

Jacob picked corn silk off his hands, hesitant to look his Father in the eye. His fidgety fingers stilled as he lay to rest the silk-draped ear of corn on his lap.

Rachael stirred her paints faster, straining to appear indifferent to the affairs of the Hoffman family. Not that she did not care. This was Roswell, her fallback boy and prime tool for influencing Jacob to her liking. Still, she loved Jacob and wanted him to marry her. Now that Roswell was gone, there was nothing holding her back.

Isaac found Rachael odious, despite his son's affection for her. He believed it nothing more than boyish lust. She often sashayed her pubescent body around Jacob like the Sirens of Jason, swaying her silken strands of hair like nets of fishermen.

She had goaded Jacob and Roswell to join the Union Army, perhaps the Confederacy, depending on her whim of the moment, all in the face of Isaac's objections to endorsing either cause. She stared at her easel and pretended to apply a wisp of red to her evening sky.

"When? Where? Is he ...?" Jacob asked, unable to complete the question.

"Afraid so," replied Isaac. "This afternoon, on the river, at Pack Horse Ford. Way I heard it, Union soldiers, scouts I reckon, saw him wadin' across the river and thought he was a Reb. They called for him to surrender; he ignored 'em; they shot 'im."

"A *Rebel?* Why, Ros weren't no more a Rebel than a chicken is a fox. He mentioned a curiosity about both sides, claimin' glory was temptin'. Me, too! Who amongst us bucks ain't! Both of us wondered what it'd be like marchin' and fightin' an' kissin' girls an' such. But *joinin'* up? Not Ros."

Rachael raised her eyebrows and resisted the urge to fling a fat paintbrush at Jacob. *Kissin' girls an' such?*

"There's more, son."

Jacob closed his mouth. He struggled to hold back tears of anger in his reddened eyes. He knew the rest of the story.

How dare Ros go pretending to be a soldier and get himself shot! Who the hell does he think he is? Fun and games are one thing, but this? The bastard! He's done gone and ruined fishing tomorrow. I was gawn shoot his rifle! Jacob's thoughts drowned his Daddy's voice, until he heard about the flag.

"He was wavin' that fool Johnny flag y'all found near the iron furnace last week, wavin' it plain as a full moon, just *darin'* 'em. That's the same as fightin' words these days. I told you so." Isaac took a breath.

"Roswell was a fine boy, Jacob, but I reckon he got what was comin' to 'im. I know Roswell wasn't a Rebel, never intended to be, I suppose, but you can't tell a Yankee soldier that whilst he's lookin' down the barrel of a Springfield pointed at the chest of a damn *fool* kid. *Damn* fool kid! This is what war *does* to folks, Jacob, and when you're fightin' your own people, well, it takes on a whole other level of hate. Hate's never meaner than with the ones we love most. I told you it'd come to this."

Anger welled up inside Jacob. Roswell was dead, his best friend in all the world, aside from Rachael, and he had his doubts about her. He paced over to Rachael and stared at her sunset painting of the Hog Trough Road and Ole Whooey's tree, of innocence and once upon a time.

She peeked at him and managed a smile, looking for a measure of reassurance. He glared at her, a scathing bolt of contempt she knew was payback for her relentless urging of Jacob and Roswell to join the army, any army, and fight like men, men in uniform.

Jacob knew his Daddy was right, but teenage pride shouted for a lashing out. He checked his rage and turned to his Daddy. His lips tightened like a dam before floodwater.

Nothing rankled Jacob more than his Father's smug pacifism. Isaac Hoffman loathed the war, all war, as was expected of any faithful Dunkard Baptist. Worse, Roswell's killing was Isaac's vindication, ammunition for his war against war.

This war was different, Jacob believed, the kind of war that demanded a stand, a personal proclamation of principles. As far as Jacob could tell, Isaac had only hollow principles, the sort of principles one flaunted unchallenged for selfish purposes at church meetings and among like-minded blowhards. Isaac's principles ended where his prosperity began.

Politically speaking, Jacob knew little about this war between the states, this dissolution of the Union, except for the banter of the valley's elders and the thunder of artillery from South Mountain. Southern troops were pouring into the Valley of the Antietam, like migrants, homeless and hungry. Sharpsburg was awash in butternut and gray that seemed to rise from the ground.

He had read the papers and the posted bills, even glimpsed the summer casualty lists over the shoulders of Sharpsburg brethren. Despite the near constant presence of either army, war for Jacob Hoffman felt like the imagery of campfire lore, not the stench of powder and blood, the waste of lives, the reality of bodies turned inside out. Lincoln vowed to preserve the Union, with force if need be, and so it was.

Union; a house divided; force; high-browed browbeating. All this hoopla seemed to Jacob like a husband whipping his wife into submission to prevent her divorcing him. *Just let the South go*, thought Jacob. *Give 'em their slaves and let 'em go!*

The issue of slavery, on the other hand, stirred Jacob's soul like nothing else. The institution divided Maryland as it had divided a nation. Isaac, a Union loyalist and Lincoln supporter, owned four. All of Jacob's attempts to understand this state-sponsored servitude only made his long walks longer and his tired mind spin for answers.

Rachael was right, Jacob knew, in her tirades against slavery, part of the reason Isaac despised her so. If the Union had a reason to take up arms against the South, perhaps this was it.

Maybe Rachael was right, too, about joining. The Sharpsburg Rifles needed men. Maryland needed protection, though from whom, Jacob was unsure. He was sure slavery needed ending.

Roswell was dead, shot by a soldier in the army of a nation bent on injecting its will, not only upon states but upon individuals as well. The equation, so simple to Jacob before, now seemed irrevocably complex.

Slavery begged resolution, Jacob understood, but he struggled with accepting one tyranny as the replacement of another. Better, he thought, to allow the South to deal with its ugliness alone.

"Come on, Rachael, let's go for a walk," Jacob said, taking her hand.

Rachael stood, her hip knocking the paintbrush to the porch, its red goo splashing on the planks. Isaac sighed.

Jacob and Rachael reached the Hog Trough Road, their favorite spot in the Valley to be alone. They walked its length, silent, pensive.

"Remember when you'd come down here and paint, Jasmine?" Jacob asked. "All day, you'd do that, an' I'd sit and wait, chewin' on grass and flingin' rocks at Ole Whooey. Let's go see Ole Whooey."

"Some of my best work was done here," Rachael acknowledged. "Remember the time Ole Whooey swooped down and picked one of my brushes, plucked it right out of my hand, like it was some field mouse? He circled his tree a time or two and dropped that brush when he realized he couldn't eat it." Rachael chuckled.

Jacob smiled.

"Why'd he do it, Rachael?"

"Because he had to."

"Because you *made* him!"

"Jacob, I did not *make* him. Ros had a mind of his own. He was just a bit too eager to act on his thoughts."

"Some of his thoughts grew from seeds," Jacob suggested. "Reckon who planted them seeds."

Rachael stared at the ground.

"John Jacob?" Rachael cooed after a few minutes of silent walk.

"Yes, Rachael Elizabeth."

"Ever notice how cherry blossoms blow to the ground, still white as snow?"

"Yes. What's your point?" Jacob asked, aware the point was secondary to her mindset. She used poetic ramblings to deal with adversity.

"People don't want blossoms to brown on the branch," she said, looking at an imaginary tree. "But they don't want them to fall white, either. Don't want 'em to fall at all, I reckon. Just stay on the tree, white, forever. I guess folks have to decide whether they're going to brown on the tree or brown on the ground. Ros blew to the ground white, didn't he?"

Jacob knew Rachael had slipped into her Miss Emily persona. It was Rachael's only way of making sense of the world. Better to nod his head, to feign understanding, than to scrunch his eyebrows.

Jacob touched her chin with a finger and gently lifted it. He brushed away her tears.

"It's okay, Rachael. I like to think Ros would have joined up anyway."

Jacob kissed her forehead and took her hand in his as they swayed arm in arm down Hog Trough Road toward the Hagerstown Pike. Rachael dampened her lips and smiled.

Jacob had been played like a country banjo, but *damn*, could she sashay!

Chapter 3

"Shhh!" urged Adonis, slouched in his shadow-shrouded chair, hands wrapped around his whiskey glass. He surveyed a congregation of Union loyalists sharing a sudsy toast in a Sharpsburg saloon.

"Talkin' about snarin' darkies is one thing," he said, volume low and eyes upon the crowd, "like braggin' about the ten-point rack you never killed. But goin' out an' doin' it, well, that's tenfold harder. They smell you."

He turned up the glass and swallowed fast his jigger of whiskey, squinted, and exhaled as if he were blowing fire. As the crowd roared at somebody's joke, Adonis slammed the glass onto the table and shook his head like a dog in the rain.

"Old Monongahela! Volcano in a bottle! Whooee!" Adonis slapped his cheek. "Like I said, a black man can smell you comin', even before *you* know you're comin'," Adonis explained, fingering the glass of its clinging drops of red-eye. "They hear you. They read your mind.

"That's where the sleight of hand comes in. These belong to Isaac Hoffman, a Union man, so he claims, who just as soon Maryland keep her slaves, or at least *he* keep *his*. Wants it both ways. Wants the protected right to own slaves, but he don't want to fight for that right. He ain't much on the South and secesh, but he sure as hell loves their ways of business. I'm going to show him another way of business. I'm going to take his slaves from him just like he took 'em from me."

"How'd he take 'em, Adonis?" Simon asked.

"Outbid me, the bastard! Had 'em bought, Claggett did too, an' the son-of-a-bitch raised the bid at the fall of the gavel. Took the whole family and gave me a smirk as he drove off in his fancy wagon, like he was King of Somalia."

"So how do *we* get hold of 'em?" Simon asked.

A beam of late morning sun spread its inexorable path across the table. Adonis tilted his slouch hat forward to shadow a scar that spanned his left cheekbone from his ear to the bridge of his nose, like a path of pink corduroy. Conspicuous scars across the face spoke of unsavory encounters, and Adonis found no value in drawing attention to that voice.

The saloon chatter buzzed and barked like the bellows of the Antietam Iron Furnace. Despite the hodgepodge and monotony of wartime banter, folks had a way of discerning the talk about slaves and slavery, like a tornado from a dust devil. He leaned closer to Simon.

"You heard of the underground railroad?"

"Cain't say that I have, Adonis." Simon gulped his beer and wiped his mouth and chin with a single broad swoop of his forearm.

"Don't that Atlanta paper you read print nothin'? Don'chu *read* nothin'? It's a network of abolitionists stretching from Florida up across the Mason-Dixon all the way to Canada. They make a way for darkies to run north to freedom. Railroad's what they call it, but it ain't no ribbon of steel.

"This railroad might be somebody's cellar, somebody's attic, somebody's closet. This railroad's the North Star and passage through the dark of night; it's painted symbols on tree trunks and lanterns on hitching posts. It's escape from bondage. It's a taste of hope. It's downright *treason* is what it is!

"Which is why *we*, as the instruments of God, have got to *sweep* these darkies off the railroad and back south," Adonis said, arcing his arm over his head. He clenched his fist around his glass, and poured another shot of whiskey. "That, and there's money to be made. A man's property is a man's *property*, even if that property *is* a man."

The revelry in the saloon continued unabated. Excitement filled the smoky air. Men and boys pushed through the swinging doors like couriers, delivering the latest rumors and gossip.

Folk knew that two great armies were gathering within a stone's throw of the village. Lee had come down by way of Boonsboro from the rumble at South Mountain and had scattered his men along the ridges east of town, within a spit of the Antietam. McClellan was on Lee's heels.

Soldiers from the South continued to pour into Sharpsburg throughout the day of the 16th, and word spread that Jackson had captured the Union garrison at Harpers Ferry.

Families were streaming out of Sharpsburg northward toward Hagerstown and southward along the Harpers Ferry Road. Talk of a great battle simmered on street corners and front porches, like summer stew. Adonis and Simon cooked stew of their own.

"Hoffman gives his slaves, especially the big one— hell, they *call* 'im Bigun—a day of freedom every week. Lets 'em go wherever the hell they please, long as they're back before suppertime."

"Sounds like Hoffman's slaves ain't exactly *slaves*," Simon observed.

"Not by Southern standards, they ain't. Like I said, Hoffman wants it both ways. He likes the convenience of

their labor, but he don't want 'em runnin' off to
Philadelphia or Lancaster or Boston or Canada. So he lets
'em run loose down here for one day a week. Lets 'em
taste freedom near the comforts and safety of home. That
way, he figures, they won't risk uncertainty in a North
growin' angrier each day with Southern victories."

Adonis paused and snickered.

"Know what else? He's lettin' the big man *buy* his
own freedom. Buyin' his freedom will do that black man
about as much good as a bible at a lynchin'. It'll take him
till the moon turns green to do it, an' then he ain't free, not
really.

"Yankee mamas are losin' a lot of their sons 'cause
of these darkies. Some up north are of a mind to just let the
South have their slaves and their country, especially after
Manassas last month. The North ain't takin' kindly to the
idea of restorin' the Union as it was.

"Anyway, if Hoffman's any kind of a businessman,
he's threatened to sell his property South if they do try to
run away. Plenty of soul drivers around these parts to run
'em down. Ain't nothin' like the specter of a Southern
plantation to straighten a darkie's hair and put white in his
eyes."

Both men laughed. Adonis downed his second shot
of whiskey and poured a third.

"Barkeep!" shouted Adonis, between coughs.
"Another bottle of this firewater!"

"How big is this Bigun?" Simon asked.

"Big enough to break you over his knee. Claggett's
the only man I ever knowed that might bring Bigun down.
We got to get Bigun before Claggett does. What I hear is,
Claggett's comin' to collect on a debt."

"So, where do you suppose Hoffman's niggers are
off to today?" Simon asked.

"I seen 'em in Sharpsburg this mornin', Bigun and
Hoffman's boy, poles on their shoulders. Bigun's family

was taggin' behind. They like fishin' in the Antietam, over at Rohrbach's Bridge. I reckon we'll head that way."

"Head *that* way?" asked Simon. "What about all the soldierin' goin' on over yonder? They's talk of a *battle*, an' it sure does look like that talk's the gospel!"

"Them people don't know nothin' about that! They'll mosey on down to the creek like it's Sunday afternoon. Talk of battle is just that–*talk!* Ain't gonna be no *battle*. They've been soldierin' around here for goin' on two years now. Ain't nothin' come of it. They're just a couple of big ol' barn roosters showin' their feathers is all."

"How we gonna catch 'em?"

"We're going to walk right up to 'em, ask 'em how's their luck–an' take 'em," Adonis replied with a broad smile of brown, cratered teeth.

"Just like that?"

"Just like that."

"I thought you said snarin' a nigger's like takin' down a deer," Simon said, confused.

"It is," confirmed Adonis, "once you got 'em down the sights of a barrel. I'd rather not do it that way. We got to make 'em think we're "deers", too. They won't see the trap 'til it's sprung."

"I'm listening," Simon said.

"We're going to wear the masks of abolitionists. Let them slaves think we're tracks on the railroad, another lantern on the line. Tell 'em we know this fine upstandin' family in Boston lookin' to take on some house servants, pay 'em wages an' all. No more sweat, we'll tell 'em. No more threats of bein' sent to the Cotton States. Cool Boston summers and a chance for some real education. Bein' house niggers sure beats the hell out of dawn-to-dusk field-farmin', blacksmithin', and barn-cleanin', even when you do get a day a week free. Let's go bag us a ten-pointer!"

Adonis slid back his chair and slapped Simon on his back. He flipped a silver dollar onto the table as they rose. The coin spun on the wood tabletop. Heads down, the two men slinked unnoticed past the chattering group. The dollar kept spinning, dizzily spinning.

A man standing a few paces back in a darkened corner of the saloon nursed his glass of beer and sauntered up to the table. He slapped his palm on the spinning dollar. The man picked up the coin and placed it in his pocket as he watched the pair leave.

Antietam Creek carved a gentle trough through rock-strewn foothills just east of Sharpsburg and in the shadows of South Mountain. Its shallow waters, swift, certain, and lean, flowed in peaceful contrast to the armies gathering near her banks. Jacob accompanied his Daddy's slaves to the creek this Tuesday, as he usually did on their 'free' days, after completing his share of chores.

Isaac Hoffman owned six slaves, two of which had died of dysentery two summers prior, and the family of four. Isaac believed 'slave' too oppressive a term, and he resented the relentless reference.

A staunch Unionist by his own reckoning, Isaac purchased his slaves from bounty hunters in 1853 at auction in Hagerstown. He outbid an unsavory gentleman by the name of Claggett Parker, paying $4,500 for the lot.

Isaac believed the purchase an act of rescue, preventing the irrevocable scattering of the Negro family. This act purchased also the undying devotion of the slaves, each preferring death to separation. Isaac justified his human holdings in the divided border state as a measure of charity and benevolence towards an impoverished, destitute people destined, if freed, for nothing more than banishment, misery, and misfortune amid an angry populace.

Keeping his slaves—"help" he called them—from the sticky hands of slave-hungry Southern coastal plantation bosses was nothing less than an act of common morality and noble sacrifice, Isaac believed. He found it a useful tool of business, on occasion, to wield the threat of their division and delivery to points south should any of them "cross the line."

These human cattle, and one fifteen-year-old son, Jacob, allowed Isaac the diversion of maintaining a lucrative wagon-making operation. Isaac carried on the family business of manufacturing farm wagons, a family tradition begun with Conestogas late in the eighteenth century.

Bigun, named such by Jacob upon seeing the man lift the rear-wheel end of a loaded Conestoga, was Isaac's blacksmith. He possessed the unenviable skill, among others, of wrapping red-hot iron rims around wooden wheels and hammering them into place.

Isaac considered the Confederate army nothing more than a bawdy band of outlaws. Beyond treason, Isaac believed, their sole purpose was the pillaging and plundering of not only his crops, cattle, and furnishings but his help as well. He gave his help three squares a day and a roof over their head, more surely than they could get south of the Mason-Dixon and probably better than fending for themselves in the free North. Isaac trusted Lincoln would not strip border states, Union states, of the right. Isaac Hoffman considered himself a savior, righteous beyond the recklessness of John Brown.

Jacob Hoffman had yet to cast his lot. He was a boy on the verge of manhood, a lad caught between the pull of innocence and the push of responsibility. Experience, however, had taught him to think, and he was not without his opinions, liquid as they were.

He viewed the Confederacy through clouded lens. States should have the right, he believed, to declare independence from the Union. Slavery, he also believed, was the work of the devil and a lesion upon human dignity.

If the South wanted her slaves, let the South have also her country. Let the lesion be severed.

The long shadows of war cast a gloom over Maryland, Sharpsburg, and the valley of the Potomac and Shenandoah, despite the successes of Lee and Jackson. Virginia played stage center in the war for Southern independence, and her resources strained to keep up. Battles at Manassas, the Peninsular, and the Seven Days had dispelled the notion of a quick war.

Christmas was a short three months away. Soldiers wondered unavoidably if the Christmas of '61 had been their last. The boredom of encampment, interrupted by brief, ferocious spurts of battle, had hardened hearts into believing the only hope for escape from the ordeal was an enemy bullet.

Southern high command, flush with summer victories at Manassas and the Seven Days, believed the time had come to push the issue northward. Late summer brought harvest time and renewed hope that Southern troops, many shoeless and lacking food, had only to replenish their bellies and haversacks for the final push to Washington and winning their country. They held fast and proud to their belief of invincibility. Such an attitude carried inferior armies to heights of superiority. The Army of Northern Virginia was such an army.

The man holding Adonis's dollar was such a man. He turned the coin between his fingers as he watched Adonis and Simon mount their horses and ride east on the Boonsboro Pike.

"Mister?" said the barkeep, tapping the man on the shoulder, "I reckon that dollar belongs to the house."

The man wheeled around and shoved a double-barreled English belt pistol against the barkeep's belly. The wide-eyed barkeep lifted his hands to shoulder height. The man said nothing as he dropped the coin to the floor and returned the pistol to his belt.

"Claggett," whispered a patron.

"Claggett? Claggett who?" asked another.

"Just Claggett, I reckon. Used to work at the Furnace. Buys an' sells slaves up in Hagerstown. Been gone four months delivering a load to a Savannah plantation. Mean son-of-a-bitch. Folks say he'd kill his mama if she come between him an' a slave deal. Wonder what he wants in Sharpsburg?"

The man reached into his pocket and pulled out a five-cent coin to pay for his beer.

"Much obliged," he said, the words rumbling from his tongue like distant thunder. He placed the coin on the bar.

The crowd disbursed piecemeal to their tables and conversations, like gusts of autumn wind through piles of leaves. The man walked away, not once turning his head to see who might be staring at him. Two Remingtons, soldiers awaiting orders, dangled on his hips. The man yanked his mount east, toward the creek, and spurred to a gallop.

Chapter 4

Jacob and the 'help' sat on a stone wall at Rohrbach's Bridge. Sprinkles of rain fell from sun-silvered clouds. Jacob heard the shadow of distant thunder and surveyed the sky. A smell filled the air, like wet cotton.

"You seen de Robert E. Lee, has ye?" Bigun asked.

"Hell no, Bigun!" Jacob said, his eyes widened by the utter improbability of such an event. "You think General Lee come all this way to Maryland to share a supper table with *me?* Best you get that grubworm on your hook an' give it a bath, maybe slap a wet cloth across your head!"

"Yassuh." Bigun baited the hook and slung his line into the middle of the Antietam.

"But, Lee, ain't he gawn need a place to hide when dese Yankees whup 'im? I figured he might come a-knockin' on yo' do'," Bigun said, after which a laugh burst from his white-teethed smile.

"You're a funny one, you are," Jacob said, smiling.

Adonis and Simon huddled among the bramble at the base of a sycamore on the bank of the Antietam not twenty paces from the bridge. Adonis slid his Colt from its hold and checked each cylinder.

"Let's catch us some slaves," Adonis said.

Moment of Truth

Adonis kissed the barrel. A flock of blue herons flapped into the air, hinting of the men's presence and splattering creek water like a summer rain shower. He tapped Simon on the arm and nodded. Both men arose and stepped from behind the scrub. They walked up the creek bank, dusting their pants, startling Jacob and Bigun.

"Gentlemen!" said Adonis with a smile and a wave. "How's your luck this fine morning'?"

Bigun noticed the long Colts strapped to their hips. He noticed also Adonis's scar and smelled whiskey in his words. Bigun shifted his eyes for a periphery view of Jacob, who had no hint of the trouble brewing.

"Just dropped my line, sir," replied Jacob. "'Spect we'll be pullin' in supper directly."

"Reckon so, young man," Adonis said, scratching the back of his head. "Reckon so. Whatchu baitin' with?"

"Grubs, bark, stuff like that. Whatever'll fool them suckers," Jacob said with a laugh.

Adonis smiled. "What's your name, lad?"

"Jacob Hoffman, sir."

"Hoffman, Hoffman. You, by chance, Isaac's boy?"

"Yes, sir. He's my Daddy," answered Jacob. "Makes wagons over in Sharpsburg. You know him?"

"Indeed. And a fine craftsman he is. Say, your– your black friend there … he wouldn't by chance be a–be a slave, now, would he?"

Jacob's smile lowered slightly. He turned to Bigun.

"This here's my Daddy's helper. He's a blacksmith in the wagon shop. Name's Jim," Jacob answered.

"You can call me Bigun, suh," he interrupted, his basal tone rolling from his lips like a snorting bull.

"My, my, indeed you are a … big-un, aintchu?" noted Adonis scanning Bigun's frame with a buyer's eye. "Well, Jim … excuse me … Bigun … if you *are* a man of bondage, how would you like to hop a train to freedom?"

"Train to freedom, suh?"

"Well, not exactly a *train*, but damn close. And freedom, certainly. Let me explain.

"Go with us, sir, and we'll deliver you to Boston, Massachusetts, to a man of considerable wealth–exporter by trade–who will promptly put you in the employ of one Samuel van Landingham, a prominent Boston attorney in the immediate need of a *paid* house servant.

"I am prepared to compensate your master quite handsomely and deliver you myself," Adonis continued, glancing over at Jacob. "Shall we begin our journey, *your* journey, to freedom?"

Bigun stared. "I'm a blacksmith, suh. I ain't nobody's house nigguh."

Adonis cleared his throat and smiled. "I'm sure Mr. van Landingham can accommodate your skills to their most advantageous use. The important thing is that you will have your freedom.

"Of course, there is some risk. What would life be without it, right? Slave catchers roam this countryside like wild turkey, and, well, much of your journey must be spent under inconspicuous cover, out of necessity, you understand.

"I presume you, Jacob, will deliver my compensation to Mr. Hoffman?" Adonis asked, reaching into his pocket to retrieve his wallet.

Simon slowly placed his thumb on the hammer of his revolver, neither man intent on paying a penny for Bigun.

Bigun glanced at Jacob and gave him the slightest shake of his head. His learned distrust for white men, armed white men in particular, heightened Bigun's sensitivity to proposals such as these. Jacob's eyes returned acknowledgement.

"Bigun ain't for sale," Jacob said. "An' he ain't interested in your–that train to freedom."

Adonis's prop of a smile fell and his eyes squinted with Jacob's resistance.

"Well, son, we're not *buyin'* him. We're merely appropriating reasonable consideration for your daddy's property. It's a personal financial sacrifice of Harriet Tubman herself. I assure you the amount will be sufficient to replace Jim twofold, maybe even get your daddy three breeders. Look, we don't want no trouble. All we want is to provide this nig–this gentleman–a way to freedom, freedom he is due in this great land. Why don't you let Jim speak for himself? Jim?"

"Name's Bigun, suh, and what Jacob says here be the gospel truth. I'm a slave, alright, but I ain't no fool. Mistuh Hoffman ain't like dem plantation bosses in South Carolina and Georgia. No, suh, Mistuh Hoffman's a hon'rable man. He owns me, true, but he treats me wit' respect an' trust. An' he's lettin' me buy my freedom."

"Fool, sir? Why, of *course* you're no fool. A man of your obvious intelligence and skills living among whites can be no fool, I assure you. No, sir, you are no fool, but you *are* a slave, the property of another man. Why do you think two mighty armies are gatherin' right here in your backyard? So they can break bread together? They're fightin' for *you*, boy," Adonis said with a jab of his finger. "Jacob, you look like a man of reason. Here's a draft for $2,000, Federal. Give it to Isaac. This is one nigger our boys ain't dyin' for."

"He ain't for sale, sir," Jacob repeated. "I don't believe slavery to be right myself, but I don't trust you men, either. Why ainchu goin' directly to my Daddy? Seems to me you got dubious intentions. Bigun here, he ain't for sale–for reasonable consideration–to nobody."

Adonis smiled and wiped his mouth. He turned to Simon. "I reckon we'll have to substitute more persuasive means, Mr. McMillan."

"I reckon," replied Simon, his hand gripping his Colt handle.

Bigun squeezed the shaft of his cane fishing pole and waved off his approaching family.

"Boy," Adonis asserted, "we're taking this slave, whether you agree to our terms or not. Now, it's in your best interest to accept this draft and kindly step aside."

A pair of eyes watched the drama from the perch of a mount hidden behind the trees on a ridge a hundred yards from the bridge. He twirled a silver dollar between his fingers and waited.

Bigun turned to his anxious family. "Go home!" he shouted.

"Bigun, we's –"

"Jesse, go home, I said! Now!"

"Wait a minute, here, Jim," said Adonis, "your family's goin' with us, with *you*. We got freedom for *all* of you."

"You is a *liar*, suh! Go home, woman!"

Bigun's family stepped backwards a few paces then turned and broke into a full uphill gallop. Simon started after them.

"Never mind, Simon!" Adonis shouted, "Let 'em go. There'll be other days."

Simon and Adonis pulled their Colts, the click of the hammers echoing across the bottomland.

"Step aside, boy. Your nigger's comin' with us."

Jacob took a step forward, to protect Bigun. Simon thrust his revolver straight at Jacob's forehead.

"I wouldn't, if I was you, boy. Simon here ain't killed a man since First Manassas, and, see, he's gettin' this *hankerin'*, if you know what I mean."

The parties stared at each other a brief moment. Jacob looked into Simon's eyes. The cold barrel of his revolver pressed against Jacob's skull.

Moment of Truth

With the swiftness of a rattlesnake, Bigun swung his cane pole, smashing Simon's wrist. The revolver flipped to the ground. Jacob reached for the gun. Bigun sent Simon sprawling unconscious with an uppercut that caught him squarely under his chin, shattering his teeth and breaking his jaw. Astonished with the quickness and strength of Bigun, Adonis pointed his pistol.

Explosions rocked the air. Adonis lurched backwards and thudded dead to the ground like a bale of hay thrown from a barn loft. Blood streamed from two holes, one in the middle of his chest and the other between his eyes. Bigun looked at Jacob, eyes as big as full moons, smoke swirling from the barrel of a revolver.

"How'd you get off two shots, Jacob?" asked Bigun.

"I didn't. I–I don't know, I–there must be someone else!"

Both scanned the undulation of the fields surrounding the creek. Simon stirred, clutching his shattered, bloodied chin as he twisted his frame and gathered his feet to stand.

Bigun bent and grabbed the revolver from Adonis's clenched fingers. Another shot cracked from the tree line. Bigun and Jacob looked in the direction of the sound. Jacob turned to see Simon on his back, a hole through his heart. A figure on a horse emerged atop the ridge and approached the pair. Jacob and Bigun dared not raise their weapons.

As the horse cantered nearer, Jacob shouted in the surprise of recognition, "Claggett!"

"Boys," the man said with a nonchalant drone and a slight nudge of his hat. "Reckon I got here in the nick of time."

Like you was followin' us, thought Bigun.

"I knew you was a good shot, Claggett, but, *hell*, that was two hundred paces if it was a *foot!*" observed Jacob.

"I'm obliged to ya, suh," Bigun said softly.

"I know these two, an' they ain't 'exactly cows in the corn," the man said, rolling Simon over with a shove of his boot. "Spect we'll be buryin' 'em around here, next to the creek where the ground's soft."

"You saved our lives, Claggett, but …"

"But what, boy?"

"Well, sir, how you gawn explain killin' 'em?" Jacob asked.

"Might be nobody'll miss 'em," the man answered. "Then again, the way I figure it, y'all owe me one. A … big-un," he said, staring at Jim.

Jacob and Bigun shifted uncomfortably. The message was unmistakable, like stepping from a rabbit trap into a stew pot. Jacob cleared his throat.

"Got somethin' to dig with, Claggett?" Jacob asked.

"Use this," the man said, pulling a tin pan and cup from his saddle.

"Ain't much to dig with, suh," Bigun noted.

"It'll do."

"Reckon the creek bank will make a good spot," Jacob said.

"You won't be needin' this," the man said, taking Simon's Colt from Bigun.

The man shoved the weapon into his belt, lit a cigar, and stooped against the stump of a sycamore tree. Jacob and Bigun scraped soil and stone, little by little, hollowing out two shallow graves. Clouds thickened and offered some relief from the unforgiving September sun. They dragged the blood-soaked bodies and rolled them into the depressions. Bigun scooped dirt over the forms. Jacob scattered leaves over the dirt.

"Finished," Jacob said, wiping his forehead and tapping the graves with his foot.

Jacob and Bigun squeezed their blistered hands and handed the man the tools.

"Nice work, boys," the man said as he rinsed the cup and pan in the water. "Now, Jacob, let me see that Colt you got."

Jacob gave the pistol to him and a hesitant glance to Bigun.

The man pulled the hammer, turned and pointed the pistol skyward and squeezed the trigger.

BLAM.

He pulled the hammer again.

BLAM.

Jacob and Bigun gave each other a puzzled gaze. The man removed the remaining balls from the cylinder chambers, flipped the pistol and, clutching the barrel, handed it back to Jacob.

"Why'd you do that, Claggett?" asked Jacob.

"Well. I'll tell ya, Jacob. See, you got somethin' I want, somethin' I deserve."

"You're talkin' about Bigun, ainchu?"

"Your old man bought him out from under these two boys here," the man said, pointing to the two fresh graves. He laughed and wiped the spittle from his chin. "Then, by god, he up an' snatched him away from me, too. This nigger's *mine*, boy, except I'm offerin' *you* your life in return. The way I figure it, I just witnessed you kill and bury two men. Three shots, three holes, and with a stolen Army Colt in your possession.

"Now, I'm takin' Bigun with me. First time it dawns on me you or your daddy are comin' after him, somebody's going to hear about you murderin' these two men. Try again and Bigun dies."

"Bigun seen what happened. He'll back me up," Jacob said.

46

"Ain't nobody gawn believe the word of a *slave*, boy!" the man said, "Anyway, Bigun's got a little matter of John Brown to think about. Ain't that so, Bigun?"

Jacob looked at Bigun. "What's he talkin' about?"

"I ain't goin' witchu, suh," Bigun declared, his feet firmly planted.

The man laughed and spit. "You ain't got a choice in the matter. Now, get movin', nigger!"

Bigun stood defiant, arms by his side.

"Nigger, I'll shoot you dead where you stand. What'll your family think of you then?"

"Spect if I go witchu, suh, I won't be havin' no family no mo' anyway. I reckon I'll be stayin' here."

The man, hewn of thick bone and heavy muscle, knew better than to attempt the distraction of a physical confrontation with the younger and quicker Bigun. He opted instead for a solution less consuming of energy and more to the point. He lifted a Remington .44-calibre revolver from his holster, thumbed the hammer, and pointed it at Bigun's head.

"Move!" the man shouted.

"No, suh!" Bigun replied.

The man stepped back at double arms-length and pulled the hammer, which clicked like the popping of knuckles.

"Last chance, nigger," the man grumbled.

"Claggett!" shouted Jacob.

"Shut up, boy!" the man said.

Bigun stared at the revolver, its cylinder filled. He tilted his head and spat.

"Bettuh dead now than go witchu."

Bigun flinched as a shot shattered the tense air. The man slumped forward at Bigun's feet, a bullet through his chest. Mouth agape, Bigun turned to Jacob.

"How'd you–"

Moment of Truth

Jacob held the Colt by his side, smoke crawling up his clothing like a morning fog. Jacob looked no more shocked than a man who had just dispatched a rabid dog.

"Percussion caps were still on the nipples. I just picked up a ball off the ground and ..."

"If he'd seen you–how'd he not *see* you?" Bigun asked.

"I was thinkin' he was gawn kill us both anyway. We were worse off me just standin' there."

Both felt relief, but neither smiled. Three men were dead, one for which Jacob was responsible.

"Best we get on home, Jacob," advised Bigun.

"Yeah," Jacob said, dropping the pistol. He watched the man's blood soak the whole of his shirt and pool on the ground. "Big son-of-a-bitch, ain't he?"

The two gathered their cane poles and began the trek up the Lower Bridge Road.

"I killed a man," Jacob realized.

"Bettuh git one of dem guns, Jacob. Might be mo' of dese up de road."

Jacob walked back and gathered the weapons, scaring off a pair of perched dragonflies. He stood for a moment and pondered the pistols. He walked to the creek's edge and flung the revolvers into the middle of the water, an overhead toss as if here casting a line.

"Why'd you do dat?"

Killing the man had clogged a crossroads in Jacob's life with a moment of truth, a point of time where no matter the decision, nothing could ever again be as it was. In an instant, innocence dissolved. Devil's darning needles.

"I don't like pistols," Jacob answered. "Too personal. Just rifles."

The killing at Sharpsburg had just begun.

Chapter 5

Jacob and Bigun crossed the bridge and left the man to collect the drifting pollen and buzzing flies. The apparent absence of witnesses suggested that families were more concerned with the signs of imminent battle than with catching supper in the Antietam.

Despite the echoes of military preparedness stretching across the shadowed valley, the area surrounding the Rohrbach Bridge retained an eerie, purple silence, like a child holding its breath before the tantrum. Bigun suggested the man's body, in the days to follow, would find anonymity among military casualties.

"I hope you're right, Bigun," Jacob said. "Ain't *no* tellin' what kind of trouble we might be in."

"You mean what kind of trouble *I* might be in. Dat back there was self-defense fo' de white man; it just plain ol' murder fo' dis nigguh."

"What do you mean, Bigun?"

"Dat Claggett gots sump'n on me. Spect he done tol' de world. Ain't no telling who knows about it," Bigun said, his voice fading to a mumble.

"About what?" Jacob asked. "You mean the auction in Hagerstown? Happens all the time. If Claggett had wanted you, he'd have paid for you."

Bigun scanned the surrounding meadows and trees and glanced back at the site of the carnage. Distance blended the bodies indistinguishable amid the brown and yellow of the grass. Crows cawed overhead, interrupting the dead silence.

Then Bigun's face stiffened. Jacob blurted something conversational before realizing Bigun had stopped ten paces back.

Above the bridge, on a bluff overlooking the creek, two silhouettes stood in the shadows of the trees.

"What is it?" Jacob asked.

"Back yonduh, on the ridge. I seen two."

"Two what?"

"People. Don' know if dey was boys or men or chillun goin fishin. But dey's lookin dat way, Jacob, towards the killins."

Jacob strained his eyes in the direction Bigun pointed.

"I don't see nothin'."

"Dat's cause dey gone now, but I seen 'em, two of 'em."

"Think they saw ... it?" Jacob asked, reluctant to give the event a name.

"I gots to b'lieve dey seen *somethin*, an' dey was lookin down on it wit' de shade," Bigun replied, looking at the morning sun.

"Could be Otto's young-uns," Jacob speculated, "or maybe his nig- ... sorry, Bigun, I–"

"Don't worry yo'sef. We gots bigger things right now."

The two tramped up the Lower Bridge Road toward Sharpsburg.

"Shit!" Jacob said in a flash of recall.

"What?" Bigun asked.

"I remember Daddy sayin he was to meet with Claggett this *evenin*, and here I done gone and *killed* the son of a bitch!" Jacob chuckled as he realized a bit of humor nestled in this turn of events.

"I reckon he'll be late," Bigun said, joining the unexpected laughter.

"Claggett an' Daddy weren't exactly drinkin' buddies, if you know what I mean. A lot of folks know how I feel about that man, too. Somebody's bound to make the connection. What if Daddy gets the blame?"

"You really think Claggett was gawn let us live? You *had* to kill 'im, Jacob. He'd a-stole *me* an' kilt *chu*, an' made it look like them other two an' you kilt each other. An' I'd done be jus another runaway nigguh."

"Wonder why?" Jacob mused.

"Wonder why *what?*"

"I wonder why Daddy is gawn meet–*was* gawn meet–with Claggett this evening?"

"Claggett be a soul driver, Jacob. You *know* that. I'm jus another nigguh he done promised to somebody else. Reckon Mistuh Isaac 'bout to sell me?"

"Naw!" Jacob replied. "I spect he's in the market to find you some help in the wagon shop."

Jacob immersed in thoughtful silence, then stiffened. A pall of realization overtook him. He had killed one man and likely another. This was not an episode of throwing eggs through Preacher Earle's window or pelting Widow Marly's cat with slingshot stones. Murder or self-defense, in Jacob's mind the distinction was insignificant.

"We got to get out of here until this blows over. We got to get you and Jesse out from here. I hear tell folks is headin for the Furnace and over to Boonsboro, even to Killing's Cave until this battle's over. Ain't nobody payin' attention to a wanderin' black man."

"Wha's yo' daddy gawn do when Claggett don't show?" Bigun asked.

"Nothin, I reckon. What *can* he do?"

"He can find another buyer is what," Bigun asserted.

"Now, Bigun, Daddy ain't about to sell you to *nobody*. You're his best worker, the finest blacksmith in the valley, an' a damn good friend. You're the reason his wagon business is doin so dadgum good. But, truth is, you're still a slave, an' we got to change that."

"He lost some orduhs lately, Jacob," Bigun revealed. "The bidness ain't doin as good as you think. I spect he's lookin to cut his losses."

Jacob looked at Bigun. "Lost some orders? He never told ... Let's stop at Renner's. Reckon what five dollars gold'll buy us?"

"You brung the coin? My, my, Jacob, if you ain't in trouble fo' killin' Claggett, you *sho'* nuf in trouble fo' takin' dat coin. It's yo' gold awright, but it might as well be gold off God's own teeth! Yo' Daddy'll skin you alive!"

"I ain't got the coin with me, but that's the least of my worries. I got credit at Renner's. Come on."

Jacob and Bigun arrived in Sharpsburg and stopped at Renner's General Mercantile.

"Howdy Jacob, Bigun! Been fishin?" asked Renner, noticing their cane poles.

"Y-yes sir, Mr. Renner," Jacob answered, glancing around at the store's shelves and tables. "Been fishin."

"Catch anything?"

"Sir?" Jacob asked, distracted by thoughts of dead men, supplies, and leaving home. "Oh, no, sir. Weren't bitin, I reckon."

"Too bad. Well, let me know if I can help you fellas, but you better make it snappy."

"Thank ya, Mistuh Rennuh, we much obliged," Bigun said.

"We'll need blankets," Jacob said.

"Whatchu talkin bout! It's summuhtime!"

"Shhhh! I know, but it might rain, and there ain't no way to know where we'll spend our nights. Let's see, blankets and … bedrolls … lamp oil … and some coffee, flour, beans … and …"

"A *wet* blanket's colduh than *no* blanket. You runnin away fo' *good?* Whatchu gettin all dis stuff fo' anyhow?" Bigun asked, eyes whiter than a Dixie barn dance.

"Bigun, you're goin with me. Now's as good a time as any, *better* than any probably, to get you off to freedom, maybe even to the Yankee army. Ever thought about wearin a blue suit and killin Rebs? Hell, you ain't got to go to *them*–they've practically come to you, right across the creek! Besides, we're in a pile of shit taller'n Piper's silo. Are you with me or not?"

"Witchu, I reckon. Yankee army, huh? Reckon dey *let* me wear de blue suit?"

"I hear tell there's a push for Negro regiments. Thirteen dollars a month. Now, help me with this stuff," Jacob said, carrying the load to Renner for tallying.

"Well, well, Jacob Hoffman," Renner observed as Jacob and Bigun plopped the goods on the counter, "if I didn't know better, I'd think you and Bigun were running away from home. Ha, ha. But then, ain't *everybody!* I reckon you're just getting ready to sit out the battle, right? Me, I'm going to be closing up in just a bit. Already boarding the windows, see?" Renner noted, pointing to a clumsy array of planks covering his north window.

"Rebels been trouncing through here all morning, most of 'em respectful enough and willing to pay, but there ain't much I can do with a fistful of Confederate notes and a mouthful of promises. Even so, I ain't about to go and tell them boys 'no', if you know what I mean. Why, some of them Rebs look like they just crawled out of a cave. Smell to high heaven and got the whiskers of grizzlies and the eyes of wolves. Most are as scraggly and lean as a pack of coyotes, eyes sunken and dark, just as ready to pounce, and breath like skunk farts. Of course I didn't *tell* 'em so, you understand, but McClellan's boys are going to give them such a *whipping*. Why, I heard that–"

"Mr. Renner ... sir ... we–we really need to get goin. Uh, how much do I owe you?"

Renner gave Jacob a courteous smile and a sigh of frustration at having been cut off in mid-sentence.

"Of course. Well, now, let's see. You're not going to give me Rebel scrip, are you, ha, ha."

"I got money. Gold," Jacob said. "It's back home, but I can run get it, pay you this evenin'."

"Well, good. Now that's ..." Renner mumbled, scribbling the prices on a scrap piece of paper. "And carry the one, ha-ha, and ... okay, got it. I reckon ten dollars even ought to cover it."

"Ten ... *ten* dollars? Let's go, Bigun."

"But wait! Jacob! What about all this stuff? Maybe I mis-added. Wait!" Renner pleaded.

Jacob and Bigun started up Main Street, passing squads of Confederate soldiers, just as Renner had described them. Jacob overheard some of the buzz from the soldiers, all of it ringing with confidence and belying the expected effects of their malnourished appearance.

Couriers raced up and down Main Street delivering messages to waiting commanders, reigns snapping side to side in mad, dust-drowning dashes. Fleeing residents hunkered to the sides of the street while the hooved storms passed.

Jacob stared at the assortment of long rifles borne by the Rebels. Smoothbore muskets; shotguns; flintlocks, even a smattering of polished Springfields confiscated from U.S. arsenals, most likely Harpers Ferry, and from the fields of Manassas.

Men hung thick blanket rolls, carpets, across their bodies, many with the swirls of ingrained designs. Jacob imagined how uncomfortable, how hot these bulky articles must be and wondered if perhaps the soldiers believed them useful as shields, their thickness the distance between life and the hereafter. He did not ask.

Some boys lacked rifles but carried instead red-bordered drums on their backs, their forage caps tilted at a swashbuckling angle, an awkward sight amid the flopping, swaying accoutrements and heavy bedrolls. They appeared more like kids on the heels of some great frolic, far from the demands and discipline, the ordinariness, of home.

The dull butternut and gray of the men contrasted sharply with the brilliant red of their flags. Some men were shoeless; others wore shoes burdened with holes and wrapped in rag patches.

Men stopped and sat on porches and propped against posts and pillars, pipes clenched in their pensive, smoke-puffing mouths.

Offbeat, contorted strains of "Dixie" and "Maryland, My Maryland" rippled through the village. Some residents unfurled the stars and stripes in utter contempt of the Southerners passing through. Others hurled insults at the soldiers, who demonstrated remarkable restraint. These men maintained the focus of a veteran army, most aware of the grim work before them.

Men drained their canteens into parched throats and onto reddened skin before refilling at residents' wells. Not a soldier among them issued a complaint. Each seemed as certain of tomorrow's outcome as they were of the sunrise.

The sunrise. *For how many would it be their last?* thought Jacob.

Jacob and Bigun reached the outskirts of Sharpsburg and the Landing Road. In a half hour, they were home.

"Gettin on, Bigun," Jacob said, observing the angle of the sun. "Now listen. Tell Jesse and the young-uns that you'll be back for 'em. One way or another, you'll come get 'em. They'll stay in the cellar until this passes. If the Rebs take this fight tomorrow, they'll take any Negroes they find, too, so Jesse's got to stay out of sight. Prepare 'em, Bigun. I'll help you make sure your family gets to freedom. I think in his heart, Daddy understands. If Daddy's losin' business, like you say, he ain't gonna need you anyhow. How much 'til you've bought your freedom?"

Bigun chuckled. "*Too* much. I reckon I gots another fo' or five years."

"So you'll pay him later. Won't be the first time he's extended credit. My guess is he'll forgive the debt. Seems perty damn ludicrous makin' you buy your freedom anyway, after all you've done for him.

"Now, the minute you see the lamplight go out in my room tonight, head for the back of the barn. I'll meechu there soon after. Right now, I'm goin' to find me a rifle to buy. I figure a Rebel'll sell me one for gold."

Bigun fought his skepticism but concluded that another opportunity this promising might never again come. He turned and headed for the barn and some chores to pass the time.

"Go on, now, Bigun. Here comes Rachael. She's been hankerin for me to shoot this here scattergun. Who the hell knows why! Funny thing about her. She loves to paint and spew poetry and get all mushy about love and stuff, but she can be the *tomboyest* thing I ever seen when her blood's up."

Bigun laughed. "I be lookin fo' de lamplight. Donchu be goin' an' getting' *yo'* blood up, ha, heh, heh."

Jacob nodded. He thought of rifles and dead men and witnesses. He hurried inside to retrieve the coin. He would have to find supplies in the house and from the barn.

****

Jacob removed the downy quilt and raised the lid. He raked his fingertips across his Mother's name,

Christina, inscribed in the white pine, and peered closely at the dower chest's shadowed contents.

His head jolted back in reflex. The musty odor of age mingled with lamplight-filtered strands of broken spider webs, swirling and floating about his face like the demons of Pandora's Box. He peeled away layers of linens and sheets and yellowed place settings–and blankets–each a reverent wedge of family history preserved like mummies. Jacob lifted the mahogany trinket box and placed it on his unmade bed.

Slight variations of color along the edges marked evidence of the careful handling of the handcrafted box. The sides were laden with carvings of arrowheads, deer, and personified exaggerations of the sun.

A magnificent horned owl relief adorned the lid, under which were cut the words "Ole Whooey – King of the Antietam Valley, 1778."

"Ole Whooey," Jacob said. "Still King."

Jacob stared at the carving. Inside the box rolled a few prized cats' eyes; a broken antler-handle knife; Ole Whooey feathers; a pocket Colt given Jacob by his Granddaddy; and an assortment of dried marsh marigolds and jasmine. The latter were the childish, lovelorn respects paid by Rachael marking events and thoughts only she would remember. Beneath this cover rested the square fold of a beige silk handkerchief.

Jacob fondled the silk cloth on his palm as a new mother would a baby in her arms. He pulled back the corners, revealing the blue embroidered letters, JJH, on top of which rested an 1838 five-dollar Half Eagle gold coin. The coin was without blemish, pure, the gleam of its essence a stark contrast to the dreariness of this morning.

Shortly before his death in 1860, Granddaddy Hoffman urged Jacob to "buy an adventure" with the coin. Isaac Hoffman insisted his son save the gold in the event of "unforeseen calamities." As far as Jacob was concerned, "unforeseen calamities" thrived just outside his door. He raised the shimmering coin from its hold, like a resurrection.

Jacob saw the coin as the fulfillment of his desires. Isaac did not have to know, not yet anyway. He pondered his dilemma as he turned the coin between his fingers and stared at its perfection. *Daddy never checks this box*, thought Jacob.

"John Jacob Hoffman, you comin' out here or not!" interrupted Rachael from the front porch.

"Comin'!" Jacob shouted, on the cusp of a decision. He shoved the wadded handkerchief, with coin, into his shirt pocket and scampered down the stairs and out the door.

Rachael held Jacob's Remmington revolver loosely in her left hand, shaking it like a scornful finger. Jacob stopped dead in his tracks.

"You gonna shoot this scattergun like you promised me?" Rachael whined, one hand on her waist and the other bent with the weight of the pistol. She tilted her head.

"Where'd you get that gun!" Jacob asked, remembering he had left it on the porch steps after last night's cleaning. "Put that *down*!"

"Worried I might pull the trigger, are you?" she said, toying with Jacob. "Relax. Look," she said, pointing to the steps.

Jacob saw the pistol's percussion caps lined along a step, like little children waiting their turn.

"Learned something new about you today," Jacob blurted, shaking his head, not sure whether to feel arousal or worry.

"What's that, Jacob Hoffman?"

"You know a thing or two about guns, that's what!"

"Anything else?"

"You're full of surprises!"

"You gonna shoot the shotgun?"

"You're an impatient thing, aincha," Jacob answered, lifting the double-barreled weapon from its corner of the porch.

"Just you shoot it, or you … or you won't get no sugar from *me*, now or at the Hog Trough," Rachael warned.

Jacob ignored her threat and rammed buck and ball down both barrels. He glanced at Rachael. He knew full well how to steal a kiss whenever the urge struck him. He took careless aim at an oak chopping stump twenty paces forward and pulled the first trigger. Rachael's clover-green eyes winced and her shoulders buckled with the explosion.

"Satisfied?" asked Jacob, lowering the gun to waist level.

The smell of spent black powder crept up Rachael's nostrils. She closed her eyes and sniffed. "Mmmm," she cooed, as if tickled by an aphrodisiac.

The shot obliterated an ear of corn wedged vertically in the stump, spitting kernels of corn and splinters of wood and scattering the afternoon lounge of nearby crows. Echoes of the blast rippled through the air, rupturing its serenity. Rachael laughed and clutched Jacob's arm.

"Do it again!" she exclaimed with delight. "The other trigger! *Pull* it!"

"I reckon not," replied Jacob as he leaned the smoking gun against a porch post and scanned the eastward stretch of Landing Road. He was keenly aware of the agitation his refusal of compliance caused Rachael.

"Why, Jacob Hoffman, I do believe you are *irritated* by my request!"

"Not irritated, Rachael," he retorted, "just manipulated."

Rachael smiled. "Then kiss me," she insisted, giggling, as she thrust forward her face, lips puckered and eyes closed, manipulation at the ready.

Moment of Truth

"In the broad of day?" Jacob teased as he turned toward an overflowing bushel basket of corn on the steps. "I got me some shucking to do, Rachael; then I got to go to Renner's for some supplies. That is, if he ain't locked his doors yet. From the looks and sounds of things these last couple of days, we might be in for a fight right soon. Best you go on home."

"Renner's? You ain't goin' to no *Renner's*, you little *liar!* He's done boarded his windows, like *that's* gonna stop them thievin' Rebels. You're on your way to Belinda Springs to lay down money on the cockfighting!" Rachael tugged the waistline of her calico dress.

Jacob wanted more than anything to kiss Rachael. Fact of the matter, Jacob longed to whisk Rachael to the barn, out of the prying sights of family, slaves, and drifters, and show her all the nuances of the kiss, as if he knew.

"I'm goin' to Renner's," Jacob insisted, touching his shirt pocket. "Wanna come?"

"What sort of fight might we be in for–right soon?" Rachael mocked.

"Yanks an' Rebs, Rachael. You *know* what I'm talkin' 'bout."

"I seen a *mess* of blue coats over by the creek yesterday mornin'," Rachael revealed, caressing the shotgun's barrel.

"The Antietam?"

"At the bridge between Newcomer's an' Boonsboro. More Yankees than the sky has stars! Then, on my way over here, I walked right through another passel on the Pike, between Miller's an' the church, only these was butternuts. Grimy lookin' predators, grinnin' *ear to ear* at me, like they ain't seen a lady their whole lives."

Still ain't, thought Jacob, a mischievous sliver of a smile on his lips.

"The ones that weren't droolin' like hound dogs, bless their souls, were relaxin'. Not a care among 'em, scratchin' out letters to homefolk or leanin' on their rifles soakin' up the air, or readin' a bible, some playin' cards or sittin' by their campfires cookin' up some God-awful smellin' stuff. Down the road a piece, another crop of 'em looked up an' noticed me. Got me some *teeth* smiles *then*. Hollers an' whistles, too. Some of 'em were right cute, Jacob Hoffman, in spite of themselves, yelpin' like field hands at a bonfire." Rachael twirled her bronze hair and smirked.

"Rachael!" Jacob chided. "What do you know about field hands and bonfires! An' *teeth* smiles, for Christ's sake!"

"Well, I got them smiles, I did! An' the things they shouted, why, I *never* … What's it to you anyhow? That's when I throwed some of Miss Emily at 'em," Rachael said, a confident lilt of one-upsmanship in her voice. "I looked 'em straight in their sunburned eyes, I did, and I said:

'Then look out for the little brook in March;
Where the rivers overflow;
And the snows come hurrying from the hills;
And the bridges often go;
And later, in August it may be;
When the meadows parching lie;
Beware lest this little brook of life;
Some burning noon go dry.'

Rachael sighed and gazed upon the sky like a wistful child.

"Got 'em thinkin'," she said with one eye closed. "They couldn't tell if I was pissin' or dancin'! Nobody turns a phrase like Miss Emily, don't you think? They looked at me like I was crazy or somethin', a lot like *you* do. I just laughed an' ambled on my sweet way.

"Seen a string of cannons, too, over yonder in Mumma's field across the Pike from the church."

Moment of Truth

"Cannons?" muttered Jacob, suddenly alert.

If phrase-turning had not shut off the urge to kiss Rachael, talk of cannons and Rebels camped as close as the Dunkard Church surely had. Shucking corn would have to wait, too.

"I gotta go. You comin' or not?"

"Not, I reckon," answered Rachael after a moment's consideration.

"Suit yourself," Jacob acknowledged, getting exactly the outcome he had hoped for. He began a brisk walk down the Landing Road. "Tell my Daddy where I've gone an' that I'll be home directly. Bigun'll be goin' with me."

"What makes you think I'll see your daddy?" Rachael shouted. "Your Daddy despises me, Jacob. You think I'm gonna stay here waitin' for *him?*

Jacob kept walking.

"Hey, Belinda Springs ain't *that* way, Jacob!" Rachael shouted as Jacob scampered down the drizzle-dampened road. "John Jacob Hoffman, them Rebs *ain't* gonna sell you no rifle, and you *ain't* about to impress 'em by takin' along a *slave*! You an' your Daddy ought to be ashamed of ownin' slaves anyhow! What I *ought* to do is to tell your daddy you got the *coin*, that's what I *ought* to do! *Renner's?* Why, you might as *well* go on to Belinda's cockfights, you liar, and throw away your money while you can! *That's* what I'll tell your Daddy, that you're about to gamble away that five dollar gold piece your granddaddy gave you, then *Bigun* if you get a mind to!"

Jacob stopped. He sighed and lowered his head.

"I'll get the basket," he droned, kicking a rock.

Rachael smiled. She had a way of getting her way with Jacob. Phrase-turning.

****

Jacob and Rachael walked the straight-line path through the Reel property, which bordered Landing Road on the west and the Hagerstown Pike at its intersection with Hog Trough Road on the east. Jacob held the basket filled with bread, butter, blueberry preserves and two flasks of water. A blanket curved around his neck. He stroked Rachael's hand, thinking about how best to reveal to her the morning's events. He loved Rachael, despite her manipulative ways. He wanted to tell her so, but on his terms, not hers.

Near the creek, Rachael spread the blanket over Mumma's soft Virginia rye and emptied the basket of its contents.

"When we gonna get married?" Rachael asked with a bluntness that stilled Jacob's heart.

"Married? What makes you think we're gawn get *married?"*

"John Jacob, there you go again!" Rachael said between chews on a piece of blueberry bread. "What was that you whispered in my ear at the cornhuskin' bee? 'Rachael Elizabeth Farnsworth, I *do* want you so, and I *do* want you to be my wife,'" she mocked, voice rising and falling, head swaying. "Of course, I'm waitin' on a more fittin' proposal, but I reckon you know my answer."

Jacob blushed. Rachael's dramatics made him feel naked, exposed. Marrying Rachael appealed to his lustful side, his need to burst out of the awkwardness of adolescence, but at fifteen, his mind of minds knew the venture was a fool's game. Silence prevailed for the remainder of the picnic.

Bread and preserves eaten, Jacob gulped his water and strolled over to the creek bank. He flung a few pebbles into the satiny water gurgling over stones and tickling the feet of dragonflies. Rachael folded the blanket and wiped the utensils and plates.

"I know what's on *your* mind, John Jacob," Rachael sang with provocation.

"You *do?*"

Rachael sauntered over to Jacob and wrapped her arms around his neck. "An' it ain't splashin' rocks in a creek."

"Well, it ain't exactly *that* that I'm thinkin' about, either."

She pulled him closer.

"I mean—what I mean is …"

"Don't talk," she whispered. She closed her eyes and kissed him. In a flash of bliss, Jacob forgot about the cannons in Mumma's fields, the gathering armies, his quest for a rifle—and the killings.

"Rachael, I—my family's *Dunkard*, an' I—"

"Shhh! I know I'm not a Dunkard, but you ain't much of one yourself. Give your Daddy time. He'll get used to the idea once he sees how happy we are. Besides, the Furnace will be hirin' soon, if it's still standin'. All the help's gone off to war. You'll have work until your Daddy simmers down an' lets you come back to the wagon business. There's a room over Shadwick's—"

"A *hardware* store? Rachael, I—"

"Shhh! I already got us dibs on it. We can—"

"Hey, boy, whatchu got there?" shouted a voice in the bramble along the creek.

Rachael and Jacob froze in surprise and looked.

"Hee, *heeee!* Now that's what I call a *fine*-lookin' woman!" shouted another. "What say we come out fer a chat, talk about the weather an' stuff."

Rachael looked at Jacob. "Got your Remmie?" she said.

"Left it on the porch."

Two Yankee soldiers, as frothy and disheveled as rabid animals, their clothes wet to the neck, emerged from the trees and brush, rifles tilted barrel toward the ground. They approached the young couple. Jacob eyed the naked Bowies each carried under his belt.

"You like these here knives, boy?" one man asked as he pulled the blade and fingered its edge. "Took 'em from a couple of Johnnies at South Mountain. Rip the guts from a bear, one stroke. Now, you don't wanna be no bear, do ya, boy? Step aside. Let some real men have a peek atchur woman."

The other man reached for Rachael's mid-back-length, breeze-swept hair. She smelled the stale pungency of his whiskey breath.

"Soft, little lady. *Real* soft. Whatchu doin' with a woman like this, boy? Not much, I reckon." He laughed.

Rachael had a mind to deliver a kick to the groin, an act Jacob fully expected. He wanted her to and dreaded her doing it.

"You–you cain't ..." Jacob started.

The other man pulled his Bowie and grabbed Jacob's arm. He placed the blade to Jacob's throat.

"Calm down, boy," he said. "We gonna whip us some Rebs tomorrow, but first we're gonna warm up. You don't wanna call no attention, now, do you?"

"Let's see now," said the soldier with Rachael, "I'm gonna take a guess as to whether y'all are Yankee Marylanders or Confederate Marylanders. Seems so hard to tell who's who anymore in this state. If I get it right, I win the *prize*. Guess what the prize is?" the soldier chuckled, stroking Rachael's hair. "And I *will* get it right."

"Boy, ain't you outa uniform?" the other soldier teased, pulling on Jacob's collared shirt. "A fine lad like you ought to *be* in uniform. Like us! Wouldja like one of these blue suits? *Wouldja?* But, then, I suspect *cowards*

don't wear no uniform." Both men laughed. "'Course, a
perty girl like you ain't got *use* for no *uniform*."

"You men!" shouted a horse-mounted officer atop
the low ridge on the other side of the creek.

Surprised, the men released Rachael and stepped
back at attention.

"Back to your posts! Now!"

The men scrambled through the neck-deep water,
rifles head-high, and disappeared into the anonymity of the
trees and brush on the hillside.

"Please forgive the insolence of my men, ma'am,"
the officer shouted. "They've not seen a female in a year,
and I suspect that was the last time they had any use for
their manners. If the battle doesn't kill them, they will be
placed under arrest. A piece of advice, if I may? The
indiscretions of my men aside, you are not on safe ground.
I strongly urge you leave the area."

"And I strongly urge *you* to control your men, sir!"
Rachael shouted in reply. "Or they're liable to get some of
my insolence!"

"Rachael! *Damn!* You gawn get us *shot!*"

"Again, my apologies, ma'am."

The officer saluted and vanished beyond the
ridgeline, his mount spanking the ground into a cloud of
sod and dirt.

Jacob and Rachael stared across the creek.

"And you wanted me to join *that* army?" Jacob
asked.

"Hold me," Rachael begged.

Jacob cuddled Rachael, her resolve at once
faltering, her head buried in the fold of his arms. The
woods bristled with lustful sounds, men uttering muffled
obscenities.

"They were there all this time," Rachael said with a
gasp of feigned surprise. "Yankee men gawking at me like

66

I was somebody's concubine," she whined, eyes dancing at the thought.

Jacob picked up the basket. "Let's go home, Rachael. War's too close."

"Marry me, John Jacob," Rachael chimed with impulse, smiling, "or one of these Yankee boys'll scoop me up, just like that," she said with a snap of her fingers.

"Rachael, there's somethin' you got to know," Jacob said with hesitance.

"What do I 'got to know', John Jacob? That you love me and want me to bear your children? That you dream of my embrace in a downy bed on cold winter nights? That your shaggy blonde hair and sky-blue eyes just about turn me inside out? That you see a long future for us filled with life and children and love, surrounded by the fruits of our dreams?"

"What?" Jacob asked, putting an arm's length between him and Rachael. "Rachael, how can you see *any* of that?"

"The hair and eyes are as plain to see as your narrow little nose, John Jacob. The rest I already know."

Jacob sighed.

"We're a nation in civil war, for God's sake." Jacob shook his head. "Listen to me! Bigun an' I were down fishin' at Rohrbach's bridge this mornin', an', well, we ran into some problems."

"What sort of problems, John Jacob?"

"The kind of problems that get a man *hanged*."

"Whatever are you talkin' about, John Jacob?"

"I'm talkin' about me an' Bigun' killed a man. Actually, it was more like *I* killed a man, maybe two."

Rachael smiled, thinking Jacob was teasing her. He did not return the smile. He stared at the dirt road for a moment and then, head down, glanced at Rachael.

"I don't like this, Jacob. Tell me you're teasin' and then ask me to marry you."

"Learned somethin' else about you today."

"What might that be?"

"Learned that when you're full of mischief an' play, I'm 'John Jacob'. When things get serious, I'm just Jacob."

"John Jacob, Just Jacob, I want to *marry* you! Now!"

"Stop with the gettin' married stuff, Rachael! Life ain't no weddin', not today! I got me a real problem, me and Bigun both.

Jacob told Rachael the story.

"That's why I cain't marry you, not now, maybe never. Bigun an' me's got to get outa here, least 'til this blows over. The way I see it, a battle is just around the corner. Maybe today, maybe tomorrow, but it's comin'. Soldiers are everywhere. Artillery's scattered in the fields. I reckon those men will just blend in with the rest of the dead once the battle starts. Cain't take that chance, though. Me an' Bigun are leavin' tonight, late."

"*Leavin'*? Goin' where? Whatchu gonna tell your Daddy?"

"Nothin' to tell. He ain't gawn know I'm gone until dinner, an' *you* ain't about to tell him *before!* I got my lucky piece."

"Your coin?"

"My Remmie, on the porch, the one you de-*cap*-itated. The coin, too, in my pocket. I still think I can buy me a rifle with it, maybe trade my Remmie and coin. Bound to be a rifle or two for sale around here by now.

"What about Bigun? He'll be a *runaway*. Lots of Southern slave traders up here just lookin' for the likes of Bigun."

"He'll be with me. Anyway, he can take care of hisself."

"You'll be comin' back?"

"Don't know. I reckon so, but no tellin' when."

Rachael's eyes reddened with tears. "Between you and Ros, a girl don't stand a chance. Why do you want the damn rifle so much anyway?"

"Ain't never had one."

"You ain't never had *me*, either. You still want *me*, Jacob? I'm here for the takin'.'"

"More'n a bee on a honeysuckle, Jasmine," Jacob whispered, kissing Rachael's forehead. "But all that's gawn have to wait. First, I got to go see about these things of a man, Rachael, *natural* things that the church won't allow me to do."

"*Natural* things? Owning a rifle is a natural thing? Does that make you a *man?*"

"I feel Ros tuggin' me, Rachael. I got to see about that, too."

"*Ros?* Am I not a 'natural thing' the church *will* allow you to do? *That* takes a man, a man of commitment, a man, by the way, who does *not run away* when life gets tough. Wait 'til *when*, Jacob?"

Jacob sighed and pulled Rachael close. "'Til I think it's safe to come home," he said. "One of those dead men was an acquaintance of Daddy's. Claggett Parker."

"Claggett Parker?" Rachael asked, stunned.

"He's been around the house before lookin' to buy Bigun. Daddy said he quit the Furnace an' took up slave-tradin'. He made a few dandy offers, but Daddy wouldn't sell Bigun. Made Claggett madder than a penned hound.

"He made a few threats, threats Daddy brushed off, but I didn't brush 'em off. I told Claggett in front of some other townsfolk there'd be trouble if he tried to take Bigun. Claggett would have killed any other man for sayin' such to his face, but he jus' laughed at me, like I was some poor alley cat.

"Now he's dead. Dead at the bridge where everybody knew Bigun an' me was goin' fishin', always do on Tuesdays. Dead with two other men. God knows who might've seen it happen, and circumstances ain't on our side."

"Folks have left town, Jacob," Rachael said. "Ain't nobody at home, except a few brave souls aimin' to protect what's theirs from hungry, scavengin' soldiers. You saw the roads this mornin'. People're on their way to Hagerstown and Harpers Ferry. Some even goin' to Killing's Cave to wait this thing out. My folks, too. Nobody cares about the likes of Claggett, and nobody seen what happened at the bridge. If anything, you did the valley a favor."

"Cain't be sure, Rachael. Bigun said he seen somebody, an' last I heard, murder's still against the law. I'll check back with you in a few days. You can tell me how the wind's blowin'."

"Your Daddy's gonna want to know where you've been those few days."

"Seems I got me an excuse just waitin' to happen," Jacob said, war in the air. "If not, I'll think of somethin'. Go on home now, Rachael."

"Can we at least take a walk through the Hog Trough. We're so close and–"

"Come on," Jacob answered in frustration, grabbing Rachael's hand, hoping to satisfy her need for blind romance.

The pair trudged through Mumma's plowed fields, stumbling among the clods of soil, occasionally falling and rising, laughing, sashaying. Jacob picked up some loosely packed dirt and tossed it at Rachael in an act of playfulness rare for him. Rachael returned the gesture, spilling the basket. The basket lay upturned in the field, forgotten.

They reached Hog Trough Road and stopped. They stared at the stretch. Hog Trough was their road, their hideaway, their place for dreaming, their factory of memories. Its trench-like appearance lent solitude and privacy, a barn without walls and doors. Here, time stood still. Here, Rachael had fallen in love with Jacob. Though Jacob did not acknowledge his heart, he had done the same. Jacob held Rachael.

Shadows stretched as the afternoon passed. Jacob and Rachael heard the unmistakable rumble of artillery coming from north of town. The mingled sounds of soldiers' shouts rippled over the fields. Military activity increased toward the Dunkard Church and on Piper's farm. Riders stretched their mounts in full gallop.

"Time to go," Jacob whispered. "Your family will be wondering where you've been off to." He kissed her cheek.

"I love you, John Jacob Hoffman. Marry me."

Jacob looked into Rachael's moistened eyes, their shamrock green glistened by the lowering sun. *She does love me*, he thought. *She does.* He hugged her and wondered might he never see her again. He wondered why he so needed the rifle. He wondered what he was really running from, running toward. He loved Rachael, but the words remained locked within his soul, like a chained spirit between worlds. He released her and sprinted toward the Hagerstown Pike and the fields of farmer Reel.

Jacob ran smack through elements of Lee's army bivouacked in the woods behind the Dunkard Church and down the Pike toward Piper's farm. Several rambunctious soldiers called, "Run, Yankee, run!"

Jacob's sprint slowed to a trot, the energy burst expended. He glanced back a time or two but saw nothing of Rachael. Ignoring the soldiers' jests, he turned and meandered back toward the Pike.

Rifles! he thought.

He felt his pocket for the gold coin. He loitered along the pike, like the dispossessed, kicking stones, gathering the nerve to ask a rebel to sell his rifle.

"Find ye a seat, stay fer the show!" shouted a lean Confederate propped against a fence rail.

"I spect not," Jacob replied.

"Suit yourself," the soldier said, puffing his pipe.

"I'll buy your rifle," Jacob blurted.

"What the hell you say, boy?" another replied.

Jacob did not repeat the question. "Nothin'. Just came to see."

"Well, ye seen. Now git!"

The afternoon slipped into dusk as Jacob gawked at the assembling mass of men and materiel.

Chapter 6

A horseman rode into Sharpsburg Tuesday evening, his sweat and dust inconspicuous among the throng of Confederates and refugees moving through town. His brother had failed to meet an expected rendezvous and was last seen milling about the saloons and streets of the village this morning.

The horseman, a soul-driver, knew the pickings were ripe for runaways and contraband. Anxious planters in the coastal cotton states awaited his return and were prepared to pay top dollar for strong bodies. He had in mind a few prized specimens in the western Maryland theatre. He needed Bronson's help for the roundup.

The horseman dismounted, stretched his arms skyward, then slapped the dust off his pants and shirt. He entered the Sharpsburg House restaurant.

"Beefsteak, rare, and milk," he ordered as he found a table. He pulled the chair back with his spurred boot and sat.

"*Milk*, sir?" the waiter asked, surprised by the request.

"Milk. White, and of cows," he replied with sarcastic clarity.

"I don't believe we–"

"Then best you find some," he said, his raspy monotone void of emotion. He stared out the window at the flurry of human traffic.

"Comin' up, sir," replied the bowtied waiter.

"I need some information," the man said.

"Help you if I can, sir."

"You seen another man that looks like me around these parts in the past couple of days?" He removed his hat, swept his hand through the gloss of his black, wavy, shoulder-length hair, and fixed his eyes upon the waiter's.

"I recognize you, sir," the waiter replied, scanning his face. "I seen you in here this morning. Why, you're Claggett Parker. Everybody knows you. I ain't seen nobody else that looks like you."

"What you seen this mornin' was my brother," Claggett said, replacing his hat on his head.

"Your *brother?*"

"From Lawrence, Kansas. He's been ridin' with Quantrill, but I need 'im more now. You gonna get me that milk?"

The waiter knew of Quantrill and Bloody Kansas. He froze in recall of newspaper accounts of the war between anti-slavery Kansans and pro-slavery Missourians.

"Would you feel better if he was a *Jayhawker?*" Claggett asked, irritated with the gawking waiter.

"I-I … Quantrill?" the waiter stammered.

"Hey!" reminded Claggett, snapping his fingers, "My food?"

"Right away, Mister Parker."

The waiter shuffled into the kitchen and soon returned with Claggett's order.

"Milk's a bit lukewarm, I'm afraid, Mr. Parker, but fresh as a junebug in May," the waiter said, smiling.

Claggett did not return the smile. He cut into his steak and nodded approval.

"Enjoy your meal, sir. Check back with you in a few minutes."

Claggett dropped his hat onto the table. He sensed the muffled buzz of conversation stirring across the diner. Word of his brother, a Confederate Partisan Raider and comrade of the notorious Quantrill, spread in the restaurant like a winter cold. He paused with a forkful of red beef at his opened mouth, and listened. Discerning nothing offensive, he shoved the meat into his mouth.

"There he is, Mr. Simpson!" shouted a small boy tugging the man's hand as both burst through the door.

Claggett chewed, startled but unconcerned, like a grazing cow.

"Pardon our intrusion, Mr. Parker, sir, but this young lad seems to believe you are ... well ... dead," Mr. Simpson said, extending his hand in a conciliatory handshake. Simpson cleared his throat. "Obviously, you are alive and well, and we shan't bother you further. A very good day to you, sir."

Mr. Simpson hustled the boy toward the door, speaking hushed admonishments.

"Wait just a minute, sir. You there, front and center," Claggett said, pointing to the boy.

The room took on the silence of a tomb as the boy paced cautiously toward Claggett. Pushing a chair out from his table, Claggett motioned with a head tilt for the boy to sit. Simpson stood motionless.

"Now then," Claggett said, "what gives rise to this exaggeration of my demise?"

The boy stared blankly, as if in the presence of divinity.

"Cat got your tongue, boy? What makes you think I'm dead?"

"I seen you shot, Mr. Claggett. I seen you kill two other men, too, down by the creek this mornin'."

"Shot? How interesting." Claggett glanced from his periphery at the eavesdropping diners. "Obviously I'm here. Tell me more of what you saw."

"Well, me an' Stump was goin' fishin' at the creek this mornin'. We seen Jacob Hoffman and his Daddy's blacksmith, Bigun, comin' towards the creek, poles on their shoulders. They come down there every Tuesday.

"Anyway, all of a sudden, two men stepped out of the bushes. Couldn't hear what they was talkin' about, but it didn't look friendly. Next thing we knew, them two men went down, shot. Then, you–that is, some man–rode down off the ridge. There was more talkin', then they buried the men, and then you–him–pointed a gun at Bigun, and then, *bam!* –Jacob up an' shot … that man. Jacob an' Bigun didn't see us, I reckon. We was hid perty good in them trees."

Claggett fixed his eyes upon the boy's.

"That's it," the boy said. "'Cept you're *here*, so that man must've been somebody else."

"Where on the creek?"

"Rohrbach's Bridge."

Claggett looked up at Simpson. "You verify his story?"

"No sir, not yet. We just figured it to be a child's babble, what with a battle brewing and soldiers everywhere and all. And knowing you were in the Sharpsburg House for supper–"

"More'n child's babble," Claggett said, as he slurped the last swallow of milk. "Milk!"

The waiter dashed to Claggett's table with a fresh glass. The restaurant's few diners craned their necks in feigned disinterest.

"That man who looked like me was my brother. Name's Bronson." Claggett emptied the milk in one mighty gulp and slammed the glass on the table. "Reckon

I'll be payin' Isaac Hoffman a visit this evening after all,"
he said under his breath.

Claggett pulled out six bits and dropped it to the
table. He handed the boy two bits. "Much obliged, boy."

"Wow! Thank you, Mister Claggett!"

"Sir, your steak?" reminded the waiter.

"You eat it," Claggett said as he exited the
restaurant. "I'm goin' after some fresh meat."

"Hmph!" the waiter sulked, out of earshot. "And no
tip."

"I'll check out the boy's story, Mr. Simpson,"
Claggett said as he spurred his mount down Chapline Street
toward the Lower Bridge Road. "You'll be hearin' from
me."

Bronson Parker joined Quantrill's Raiders in June,
1862, in allegiance to his firm support of the Confederacy
and to his belief the Kansas Territory's destiny was slave
statehood. An expert marksman, Bronson had mastered the
art of guerilla warfare, facts inconsistent with his killing at
the hands of a teenage fisherman.

Claggett's junior by five years, the twenty-eight-
year-old Bronson had declined Claggett's invitation to
participate in John Brown's raid on Harpers Ferry in 1859.
His heart and sympathies were Southern.

Claggett had delivered a load of muskets and pikes,
under the cover of Antietam Iron Furnace nails, to Harpers
Ferry the day of the raid. He intended to rendezvous with
Brown during the predawn hours before the raid, but a
broken wagon wheel delayed the delivery. Unwilling to
risk capture and hanging, Claggett abandoned the load
behind the armory and blended in with the citizenry.

The lure of profits from the slave trade trumped his
hollow convictions and thirst for glory. Instead, he
appeared no more than a curious bystander to the failure of
Brown's raid and awaited his opportunity. His wait was
short. There, he saw Bigun.

Moment of Truth

Jim "Bigun" Pemberton had been Isaac Hoffman's blacksmith since 1850. His dexterity with fashioning iron rims around the wood of wagon wheels, as a musician might create the perfect mix of pitch and duration, earned favored status with Isaac. Bigun forged his virtual freedom and made himself indispensable to the success of Hoffman's wagon trade.

Isaac had won a lucrative contract with the Antietam Iron Furnace in 1855 to manufacture and deliver one hundred wagons in two years' time, a wagon every week. The wagons were used by the Furnace to transport iron ore offloaded from barges floated up the creek from the Potomac River, as well as the delivery of pig iron, nails, coke, and an occasional artillery tube.

During this period, Claggett worked at the Furnace as a filler and had frequent contact with Isaac Hoffman and Bigun, a slave he had long coveted and had tried once to purchase.

As the melee of John Brown's raid unfolded, Claggett set his sights on Bigun, one of a handful of uninjured participants with Brown's raiders. The final assault by Lee's men on the arsenal at Harpers Ferry ended the raid and put to rest any organized slave uprising east of the Mississippi.

Bigun, unknown to locals, managed to evade his pursuers, with Claggett's help, across the Potomac into Maryland and back to Sharpsburg.

Tempted by the good fortune of events, Claggett instead returned Bigun to the Hoffman farm with the promise never to reveal Bigun's whereabouts on that fateful day. In return, Bigun agreed to "run away" into Claggett's possession three years after the raid, as long as he agreed never to send Bigun to the Deep South. Claggett had come to collect on a debt Bigun had long forgotten.

Now an eight-year-old boy had linked Bigun and Isaac's son to Bronson's death. Claggett intended first to unravel the riddle of this turn of events.

Night fast approached. Claggett encountered Rebel soldiers preparing the lines for tomorrow's inevitability. As Claggett approached the Rohrbach Bridge, he noticed Rebel activity around a few prone bodies several yards across the bridge. Identification of the bodies from his vantage was impossible. Confederate pickets stopped Claggett and turned him back before he could get across the bridge.

Frustrated, Claggett returned to Sharpsburg, an eerily quiet, darkened village. The town seemed like a child quaking behind a banister while his parents argued. He walked the deserted streets looking for signs of Bronson, hoping the boy's account was indeed imagination.

Finding nothing, Claggett pulled each of his three Colt revolvers, spinning the cylinders and confirming the loads. Good fortune intervened once again. Distractions were bountiful; witnesses were nonexistent. Giving a gentle kick to his mount's sides, Claggett trotted toward the Landing Road and the Hoffman residence.

Chapter 7

The valley air diffused the twilight like the satiny amber of spilt whiskey. Ole Whooey poked his head out of a hole in a chestnut tree on the northern edge of Piper's cornfield. His yellow eyes surveyed a landscape split by parallel ruts, Hog Trough Road, a divider between the Piper and Roulette farms.

Rodents and rabbits scampered through rows of corn and fields of grass. The owl jumped to a nearby branch. Silhouetted against the western sky, the blood-red sun half-sunk, Ole Whooey began his hunt. The melancholy of his call rolled on the air like an omen. Cicadas and whippoorwills joined this resonance of dusk.

Bats darted, defying physics, as if filled with the Spirit. Ole Whooey sprang from his perch, the spread of his six-foot span in full glide. Prey scattered like buckshot through the fields and across the depths of Hog Trough Road. Escape was brief, futile. Life and death exchanged bows, and so began the dance.

Sharp exchanges of artillery north of town, armies posturing for the contest, gave notice the moment of truth was at hand. Jacob stopped to listen.

Residents, the few remaining, heard and waited.

The sky dimmed.

Lamplights lowered.

The flicker of candlelights dwindled.

Heads lay on pillows and crates, but few slept.

The valley, one eye opened, wilted into darkness. Jacob took a deep breath for the final sprint home.

Ole Whooey returned to the chestnut branch overlooking Hog Trough Road and peered with patience, as he had done night after night, the limp catch ensnared in his talons.

Jacob skidded to a halt on the dirt lawn at the foot of the porch steps. He bent over, hands on hips.

"Where you been? Mistuh Isaac come back a while ago. Prob'bly good you was gone. Said fo' us to come d'rectly over to Mistuh Samuel's place."

"Samuel's place?"

"Said he needed to talk to you an' me 'bout somethin'. Reckon ... he knows?"

Jacob considered Bigun's question.

"Dem Rebs done run off Mistuh Samuel and Miss Lizzy and all eight of dem young-uns. Mistuh Samuel and a couple of his boys and yo' Daddy is goin' back to de house dis evenin' to try to salvage some food and valu'bles. I 'spect de house'll be all tone up by den."

"Had to–had to take a walk with–with Rachael," Jacob said, panting. "She can be a *dadgum* pain when she–she sets her mind to it. Where's the Mumma family stayin?"

"At the chu'ch, I reckon. Yo' Daddy, too," answered Bigun. "He says it'll be de safest place. Don't know how he knows dat. I know he 'spectin' us."

"Daddy's stayin at the church?" Jacob asked, surprised. "Had his talk with God, I spect."

"Mistuh Isaac sent Jesse an' the young-uns wi' dat Missy Rachael's mama over to Killin's Cave. What I gawn do now, Jacob?"

Jacob pondered this turn of events.

"We ain't goin'."

"We ain't goin'?" Bigun asked. "We's *stayin'?*"

"No, not stayin', neither. We ain't goin' to Mumma's."

"Ain't goin' to Mumma's? Whatcho Daddy gawn do when we don't show up?"

"I don't know, but we cain't go worryin' 'bout that now. We got enough pigs at the tits as it is. We'll be back in a couple of days. By then, Rachael will know if word's out about Claggett and them other two. Meanwhile, I know where we can find us the best seats in the house for one dandy of a fight. Don't you *wanna* see a battle? You're comin' with me."

"I spect," Bigun reflected. "I gots a mind to pick me up a rifle and shoot some Rebs myse'f."

"I don't reckon that'd be such a good idea, Bigun, if you want to see your family again. Maybe we ought to scoot on around this fight so you won't go gettin' your blood up."

"Missy Rachael's mama done lef' you some food in the kitchen."

"Bless her heart! I thought I smelled a slice of Farnsworth heaven."

Jacob and Bigun made their way to the kitchen and sat. Bigun guzzled a goblet of milk and shoved a tall lard biscuit into his mouth. He hunkered over his plate, like a stray dog over a bone, before it occurred to him he was eating at a white man's table. He stopped in mid-chew; his guilty eyes shifted toward Jacob, as a child caught with his hand in the cookie jar.

"Scuse me," he mumbled, crumbs spilling from his mouth to the floor.

"For what? *Eat*, man! Black man's gotta eat same as a white. If anybody deserves to eat from this table, you do."

"I's talkin' 'bout my mannuhs."

"Oh. Apology accepted."

Jacob grabbed a biscuit, pressed it into his mouth, crumbs falling, and smiled.

Bigun prayed. "Thanky, Lawd, for de bounty of dis table. Be wit Mistuh Hoffman as he he'ps doze in need. If dey's a battle on the morrow, be wit doze what's fightin' fo' the cause of freedom. In the Blessed name of *Jesus*, Amen."

Both grinned and made dibs on large portions of biscuits, milk, corn on the cob, sidemeat and a tub of white gravy.

"What's this?"

"A note from Missy Rachael. Her mama say it explains takin' Jesse an' de chillun to de cave."

Jacob took the note and read it. "Hmm." He tossed it onto the table.

"More of Rachael's gibberish. Weird, ain't it?" Jacob observed.

Bigun split a biscuit to make a sidemeat sandwich. "I don' rightly know whatchu mean, suh."

"This house; this valley; this *age*. A nation at war with itself, and here we are in the thick of it, a white man an' a black man eatin' biscuits side by side from the same table.

"This war ain't just in the newspapers no more. It's right outside our doors. You an' me in this house, by ourselves, at night before a battle that we get to *witness*. We're on the edge of *history*, Bigun, *literally!* I got me a feelin' 'bout all this. Don't this sorta make your skin all bumpy?"

"Makes a *white* man's skin all bumpy. Mine's still sweaty, an' it will be as long as I's a slave. No offense to you, Mistuh Jacob. I appreciate what Mistuh Isaac does fo' me an' my family. I appreciate what you's 'bout to do fo' me. It's jus' dat—it's jus' dat dawn never comes fo' a slave. As long as whip and shackle meet black skin, ain't none of us free, not even you."

"Jacob. Not *Mister* Jacob; not *sir*. Just Jacob. No offense taken, Bigun. We're gettin' you outa here, your family, too. Funny, though. Daddy's gone; Rachael's gone; your family, gone. We're here. Ain't *we* the ones supposed to be gone?"

"My fam'ly, Jacob; what I gawn do?"

"They'll be fine, Bigun. If they're with Rachael, they're in good hands. Then again, sometimes I think bein' throwed into battle nekkid would be a more pleasin' experience than bein' with Rachael. Least in a battle, a man can shoot back or play dead," Jacob said, smiling. "Gettin' dark. Let's finish this and get ready.

"Whatever food's left, pack it," Jacob continued. "Wrap some of these melons in sheets, along with that ham and a couple of pounds of sugar and beans. Heck, get anything we can carry an' eat. Rebs'll sure as shit take *all* this, unless we take it first."

"Yanks, too?" Bigun offered.

"Yanks *especially*."

"Who de good guys be?" Bigun asked.

"Ain't none, I reckon," Jacob pondered. "Lincoln?"

"An' Frederick Douglass," answered Bigun.

Jacob and Bigun spent the next few hours stuffing away valuables into the cellar and packing essentials for their journey.

Jacob knew the relative positions of the armies. The Yankees occupied the east side of the Antietam; the Rebels, the west side. The Confederates, he believed, possessed a material disadvantage, geographically. The Potomac River snaked to their backs, not three miles from Sharpsburg. While safe behind Rebel lines now, the Hoffman house lay in direct line of a Southern rout.

Artillery rumbled on occasion north and east, feeler shells sent forth. Spatters of distant small-arms fire suggested a bulge of tension ready for the breach. Jacob stopped, a load of silver in his arms, and listened. Amid the grumbles of frogs and the chirps of crickets, a gigantic eruption of flesh simmered at the point of boil.

"We best get a move on, Bigun," Jacob urged. "If I'm gonna get me that rifle, I best be doin' it before dawn. We got us a whole army to get through, maybe two. Besides, Daddy'll be sending after us soon."

Jacob shoved his Remmie between his belt and pants. He patted his pocket for his coin, his adventure. Both picked up their burdened packs and started out eastward on the Landing Road toward the Reel farm.

A shroud of clouds kept the walk as dark as a cave. Gunfire had died down. The nocturnal owned the fields now. Only Jacob's and Bigun's blind familiarity with the terrain prevented utter disorientation. Ahead, the sound of a galloping horse grew louder.

"Off the road, Bigun!" Jacob said.

The two slouched in scrub brush along the roadside and waited.

"Rebs?" whispered Bigun.

"Not unless they got the vision of Ole Whooey."

The horse sprinted by, scattering rocks and dirt, and disappeared in the grainy gray. Jacob strained to make out its rider.

"That's one of Mumma's, I b'lieve," said Jacob. "Daniel or Sam, Jr. Daddy's sent somebody out to find us. Come on. Let's go."

Jacob thought about what might await them. The whole Southern army was bivouacked along the Hagerstown Pike and in the woods behind the Dunkard church and in Mumma's and Piper's fields. As they approached the farmhouse of farmer Reel, the chatter of a great volume of men grew clearer. The pair was several hundred yards southeast of the church.

Jacob guessed the time to be around 2:00 a.m. Activity swirled near the Reel farm as soldiers ate rations, played cards, wrote letters, sang songs, and conversed.

Some soldiers, firm in their belief this was their last night
on Earth, meandered about like lost children, pensive,
staring at the heavens, hands in pockets or clasped behind
them.

A group of pickets stopped Jacob and Bigun at the
intersection of Reel's farm lane and the Landing Road.

"You fellers civilians?" asked a soldier.

"Yes, sir," answered Jaocb.

"Oooo. Did y'all hear that? 'Yes, sir.' "Whatchu
got in them packs? Smells awful good."

"Stuff."

"Stuff? What ... stuff?" the soldier pried, reaching
for Jacob's pack.

Jacob pivoted to avoid his reach.

"Hmm. Where y'all off to this time o' night,
anyhow?"

"I live down this road, that way," Jacob said,
pointing. "This here's Bigun. He works for my Daddy."

"A slave?" asked one of the soldiers.

"'Fraid so," answered Jacob. "Not for long,
though."

"Tha's yer choice, I reckon, but don't be sayin' that
around here much. Some of these boys have been th'ough
the devil an' back fightin' for somebody's right to hang on
to these darkies. Others, well, hell, they don't give a shit
'bout nothin' 'cept killin' Billies."

"Billies?"

"Yanks. Blue Bellies. Devils. So, where y'all
headed?"

Jacob and Bigun looked at each other, neither sure
how to answer his query.

"That way," Jacob answered, pointing northwest
toward the obscurity of darkness.

"Whatchu gawn do, *watch* the fight? I reckon
you'll have yourself a front-row seat that way. I got me a
better idea," the soldier offered.

"What dat be," asked Bigun.

"Gen'ral Lee wants Maryland boys to join the Army of Northern Virginia," the soldier answered. He eyed Bigun. "I 'spect he'd just as soon take runaways as scraggly white trash. All you need is a musket and some cartridges. They's a couple of regiments up yonder short of men. Bound to be an adventure. Interested?"

Jacob heard the magic words: 'musket' and 'adventure'.

"A musket? For *free?*" Jacob asked like a schoolboy in a toyshop.

"Jacob, we ain't here to fight," Bigun said.

Jacob cleared his throat.

"Right, well … I'll think about that … mighty fine offer," he replied to the soldier as the pair turned and set off through the bramble of Reel's fields.

"Better armed than not!" shouted the picket. "Don't matter no way. You both gawn get bit, wadin' into a snake pit like that!" The soldiers let out a cackle and hollered some obscenities.

"Where you reckon the chu'ch be, Jacob?"

"'Bout a half mile or so through yonder," he replied. "Ain't but a smudge of light to go by. 'Spect they don't want them Yanks drawin' no bead on 'em or findin' cannon range.

"Dey lookin' fo' mo' soldiers, Jacob. Dey gon' take us in, th'ow us a rifle an' a bag of bullets, an'–"

"I know, I *know*." Jacob was as certain of getting his rifle as bird dung on a Sunday suit. He was prepared to give his five dollars gold, Remmie as well if he had to, but the asking price of enlistment was a trifle more than he was willing to go. "Let's camp here."

"What say?" asked Bigun, surprised by the sudden change of plans.

"I think we ought to camp right here, that's what."

"Is you an' yo' senses parted comp'ny?"

"Look, Bigun, if we go farther, we're bound to run across some soldier who'd just as soon cut our throats as look at us. Did you see the look in that feller's face back yonder? We're lucky they didn't eat our food an' shoot us as spies. No, let's get us a little shut eye right here an' see what happens come light."

"You de boss, but I ain't likin' dis one bit. Why don' we jus' go on over to Mistuh Samuel's place, take our chances wit' Mistuh Isaac."

"Same thing, Bigun. We'll have to cross as many Rebs that way as this way. Let's just see what happens," Jacob decided, unpacking his bedroll and blanket.

Bigun sighed and followed suit.

The two laid down on a grassy mattress, wadded shirts for pillows, and stared at the heavens. Jacob brushed a night crawler off his chest. Clouds had parted, leaving jagged holes across the canopy of infinity. A falling star sliced across the northeastern sky, its trail etched into Jacob's brain. Two more streaks followed.

"You see that, Bigun?"

"Sho' did."

"Damn perty, them things, when you can see 'em. Sneaky as possums in daylight, though," Jacob mused, smiling. He thought of Rachael.

"Or bullets in battle," added Bigun.

Jacob's smile receded. He closed his eyes and thought about the thousands of soldiers who had just seen the same shooting stars.

Chapter 8

The more Claggett thought about the boy's story, the angrier he became. He held little doubt as to the story's veracity. He pondered what to do about it. Bronson was dead. Revenge was alive.

Claggett Parker was the Paul Bunyan of the east. Most men smelled like Claggett, sweaty and skunk-like, but few tread this earth with similar physical characteristics, Bronson once the rare exception. Barrel-chested and arms like oak stumps, Claggett was the reigning arm-wrestling and bare-fist-fight champion of all of western Maryland. Few men dared challenge his physical prowess, and those who did seldom made the same mistake twice.

Still, one other man possessed the strength, and the balls, to go toe to toe with Claggett if need be. Bigun was not stupid enough to start a brawl with Claggett but was fearless in the need of self-defense and the defense of his family.

Claggett craved the money he could command for such a specimen of manhood as was Bigun. Claggett believed he possessed the proper mix of motivation, meanness, and manliness to tame Bigun and take him to Charleston. Preston King, owner of vast tracts of rice; cotton; and cane sugar along the Cooper River, awaited the delivery.

Moment of Truth

The countryside along the Landing Road was dark, foreboding, like a keg of black powder sitting on a stove fire. It was a rolling no-man's-land of anxiety. Claggett galloped past the Reel farm and turned left. Midnight had come and gone, and the time was ripe for raiding the home of Isaac Hoffman and collecting his debt.

Claggett stepped with eagerness into the probability of killing Isaac and Jacob. He had reason enough, he believed. Isaac had snapped the rug out from under Claggett's attempt to buy Bigun, and now Jacob had killed Bronson. He would put a bullet into Bigun if worse came to worst, but killing him was out of the question. Damaged goods heal; dead goods rot.

As his horse sprinted toward the Hoffman home, Claggett perceived the sound of a cough. Pulling reign, Claggett stopped the lively mount and listened. Owls hooted. Squirrels tramped through leaves.

"Hooves," he concluded, as he jerked the horse's head, spurring him onward. "Or my imagination."

Isaac's home was an empty, lifeless shell. Claggett kicked in the front door, pistol drawn. Finding a lantern, he scratched a match. He searched every room. He found the remnants of a meal the only evidence of recent occupation. He caught glimpse of a note on the kitchen table.

Dear Jacob,

Have taken Bigun's family with mine to Killing's Cave to wait out the battle.

Be careful, my sweet. This incident at the bridge will all blow over, as will tomorrow's fight, and I will have you in my arms again.

In my heart, I know you love me Jacob, though you struggle to say the words. No matter. I feel your heart speaking, as Poe wrote:

"But our love it was stronger by far than the love
Of those who were older than we--
Of many far wiser than we-
And neither the angels in Heaven above,
Nor the demons down under the sea,
Can ever dissever my soul from the soul
Of the beautiful Annabel Lee."

Until I see you again, I remain your devoted
Rachael.

"Killing's Cave, eh?" Claggett said. So Bigun's
with Jacob. Let's see what a little bait can do to draw him
back."

Claggett wadded the note and dropped it to the
floor. He grabbed three biscuits, sat, and penned his own
note. When he finished, he folded it, shoved it into his
buckskin pocket, and exited the house. He thought for a
moment of torching the place. Rethinking, he mounted and
set off for the cave via Snyder's Landing.

Claggett knew the trail to the cave and could
traverse it blind if need be. Ahead, he saw flickers of
torches and campfires and heard the muffled chatter of the
assembled refugees. Firelight cast sputtering shadows on
the cave entrance, a broad arch overlooking the Potomac
River and the Chesapeake and Ohio Canal.

Tying his horse to a branch protruding from the
rock cliff, Claggett sat on a boulder, like a spider in the
recesses of its web, and observed the wandering masses,
awaiting his prey.

"Excuse me, sir. Can you spare a match?" asked an
elderly man, clutching a cane in one hand and a cigar in the
other.

"Here ya go, old man," answered Claggett, striking
the match and touching it to the cigar. "Gonna be a bigun."

"I spect. Cain't never tell 'bout these things," the old man grumbled between draws. "Little Mac's got hisse'f an army that'll whoop ol' Lee for good."

"You don't think Lee can take 'im, old man?"

The man squinted one eye and stared at Claggett. "You're a perty big ol' boy, yourself. I reckon *you* could take Lee." The man wheezed a laugh. "Have you forgotten about Malvern Hill?"

"Have *you* forgotten about Manassas?" Claggett countered, drawing his Bowie knife and grabbing a green stick felled by a storm. "Short memory, old man. Barely three weeks ago."

"Hmph! I reckon the Union learned its lesson. McClellan will do to Lee what your Bowie's 'bout to do to that stick," the man answered and ambled away toward the cave, pecking his cane upon the ground.

"Wait a second, old man!" Claggett called. "Let me ask you something."

The man walked back, puffing the cigar dangling from his mouth, looking more like a dilapidated locomotive than a spent human being.

"What is it?"

"I'm lookin' for somebody. Hopin' you might be able to help."

"Try to."

"I'm lookin' for Isaac Hoffman and that big ol' blacksmith of his."

"You mean Bigun? Hell, ain't seen neither one of 'em. Jacob, neither. I figure they're stayin' with the house or headed over to the Furnace. That's where most of Isaac's business is these days. Sorry I cain't he'p ye none."

"That's alright, old man. You go find yourself a comfortable place. I reckon you're gonna be here a day or two," Claggett said, whittling his stick.

"*Have* seen Bigun's family," the old man revealed.

"Oh, yeah?" Claggett asked, pretending indifference.

"Yep. Up yonder by the cave entrance, next to that cook fire," the old man said, pointing. "They might could he'p ye."

"Obliged." Claggett glanced up the hill and discerned three dark forms huddled against the exterior cave wall. "Bait," he muttered.

"What's that you say?" the old man asked.

"What? Oh, nothing," Claggett said, shaving green strips off the stick. "Just thinking out loud. Thanks again, old man."

Claggett shoved the Bowie into its scabbard. He stood and approached the group of three blacks, a woman and two male children.

Rachael brought over a tin cup of water and a loaf of bread. She handed it to Jesse, who gave it to her famished, thirsty children.

"Thanky, Missy," Jesse said in a tone of resignation, eyes reddened with tears of worry. "Reckon where my man be dis night. You s'pose dem Rebs done foun' 'im? Oh, *Lawd*, he'p 'im!"

"You calm down, Jesse," Rachael whispered, wrapping her arms around her. "Jesus has got Bigun right where He wants him. Jacob, too. They'll be all right, you'll see. I'm going to go get us more bread and water. You'll be fine here."

Rachael picked up a torch from the cook fire and set off for the riverbank. Congregations of townsfolk handed food and water and offered blankets and other assistance as needed.

"Miz Pemberton?" Claggett said with the gentleness of a preacher.

"Yassuh?" Jesse answered.

"Miz Pemberton, may I have a word with you, please?"

"'Bout what, suh?" Jesse asked, clutching her two children, wary of the giant man's deceptively soft tone.

"About Bigun, ma'am."

Jesse's ears opened like flowers to a bee. "You know where he be?"

"I know, Miz Pemberton, and I can take you to him."

"Where my man be, Mistuh ...?"

"Parker, ma'am. You and your children need to come with me and I'll take you to him."

"Is he okay? I mean, dey ain't kilt 'im, has dey?"

"He's fine, Miz Pemberton. This way, please," Claggett spoke, like a salesman of snake oil, glancing toward the riverbank, ever watchful for a returning Rachael.

Claggett spotted the old man, still puffing his cigar, lounging on a stump near the cave entrance.

"Wait here, ma'am. I'll just be a moment," he told Jesse.

Trotting over to the old man, Claggett reached into his pocket and pulled out a folded piece of paper.

"Do me a small favor, old man?" he asked.

"If I can, and for three cigars," he replied.

Smiling, Claggett handed the man five cigars and some matches. "Give this note to the prettiest young lady you see here tonight."

"A big, strong, handsome man that you are, and you're afraid to give it to her yourself?" the old man teased.

"Not afraid, old man. Just busy. Here, take two more cigars. Yonder she comes now," Claggett said, pointing to Rachael struggling up the hill, pressing foodstuffs and a torch against her body.

"Hmmm. Picked yourse'f a *peach*, ya did," the old man said, turning. Claggett was gone.

Claggett, Jesse, and her children stepped past the cave entrance, chattering folks inattentive to their presence.

Just then, Rachael returned with more bread and water. She noticed Jesse and her children walking toward the road with a mountain of a white man pulling the reigns of a horse, shadows spreading like spilled oil. She knew of only one man in the valley capable of blocking as much light. The bouncing waves of his hair sealed his identification.

*Claggett? That's **Claggett Parker!** She thought. The bastard's **alive!** But how?*

"Ma'am?" the old man said.

Rachael turned around. "Yes?"

"A man asked me to give this to you. Big man. Make a fine husband to a filly like yourse'f."

"Take the torch, please?" Rachael asked.

The old man took the torch and propped it against the cave wall. Rachael set the bread and water on the ground and took the note. She turned, but Claggett and Jesse had vanished into the darkness. She dared not pursue them now or announce their departure for fear of what Claggett might do to them. She unfolded the paper and read the scrawl.

> "Have Jesse and children. Will exchange all
> for Bigun. Deliver to Rohrbach's Bridge
> noon of September 24. Tell no one, bring
> no one. No weapons. If instructions not
> followed to the letter, all will die. – CP"

Rachael crumpled the note and walked to the road. She stared down its blackness.

Chapter 9

"I got the guard," announced a private come to relieve Bull. "Vittles on a fire, down-ridge, behind a little white buildin' yonder, church, I reckon. Some of Hood's boys killed three or four hogs and rounded up a mess of corn ears an' sweet taters. Farmer's cussin' like a street whore, says he cain't whoop us hisself but them Yanks sho' nuff will." The private snickered and wiped his forehead with his backhand as he propped his smoothbore against a maple. "Madder'n a picked tick, he is. Best eatin' I had since Selma. You better git on after them fixins."

"Obliged." Bull stuffed the folded notepaper and a stubbed pencil into his pocket. He came to his feet and grabbed his rifle and cartridge box.

The two men stared across a fallow field toward a mass of woods some six hundred yards east northeast. The private fondled images of glory and invincibility, like a baby after a mobile in a crib, while Bull pondered an outcome more realistic, more immediate and final.

"I hear Mac's ego's 'bout as big as his army?" the private observed, gazing into the black toward the few dots of light scattered like stars along and above the meander of the Antietam.

The action of an hour ago had petered to an occasional spurt of blind musketry. The armies surrendered to the deceiving calm of darkness.

"Pride goeth b'fore a fall, my Mama always tol' me." The private sighed, hands cupped over the muzzle of his musket. "Bet them boys is eatin' biscuits and gravy right about now, reckon? Laughin' and singin' and carryin' on like they ain't got a care in this world." The private shook his head. "All I got to say is they best get their bellies full, 'cause t'morrow's the day we gawn kick some Yankee ass. Gawn be quite a show. Yes sir, *quite* a show. Poague's done set up his guns on a hill b'hind them trees yonder. Lee's batteries are down the line a piece. We got the high ground and they got t' cross open fields. The way I see it, target practice."

"Quite a show," echoed Bull in the stoic, faraway monotone of experience as he began his trek rearward. Bull stopped and turned toward the private. He opened his mouth to speak but hadn't the verve to dress down the private's simplistic view of battle. The private would find out soon enough and in terms far more lurid than Bull could impart.

Bull continued down the road. The pork, corn, and sweet potatoes, a feast by Rebel standards, fed a fantasy of plenty and was, itself, worth the coming fight. Bull was off to get his and was mindful to shoot any man, Rebel or Yank, who tried to stop him.

The private, meanwhile, fingered the two and one half pounds of lead in his cartridge box. *Forty rounds ought to be plenty*, he thought. *Whoop 'em b'fore noon.*

Full of the immortality of his enthusiasm and the glory of his coming kills, he mopped the slime of sweat and dirt from his hairline and smiled toward the unseen enemy.

Bull scuffed his blistered feet along a cow path adjacent to the Hagerstown Turnpike. Most of the day had been spent marching the seventeen miles of hills, rocks, and roots from Harpers Ferry. The Pike swarmed with clusters of stragglers searching for their command, their leisure interrupted by the staccato of probing musketry and the thunder of couriers galloping past. Bull paused and watched the urgency of the preparation. He had seen it before. Like crazed ants, officers scurried men and equipment from point to point.

Rebel cook fires dotted the depths of woods and ridge lines as far as Bull could strain his dusty eyes to see. Rations, what few existed, disappeared with the haste of carrion before the lion. Most of Lee's army had not eaten a sit-down meal for days. Company commanders shouted orders ignored. Men lay down their heads on the damp cotton of bedrolls. Bull made his way past a white square building atop a knoll alongside the Pike. Regiments of Confederates teemed around and behind the structure.

Must be that church, Bull thought. "Sixth Alabama?" he shouted above the din of chatter and the clanking of arms and accouterments echoing through the trees.

"Down yonder!" a man replied, pointing south toward Sharpsburg. "Five or six hundred yards they's two roads to the left! Take the second one. The Sixth is bivouacked in some corn and apples, lucky dogs. Prob'ly done et 'em all by now. You'll see the fires an' the colors."

"Obliged," Bull said.

Bull Stokes found the Sixth, and Sergeant Teaseley, bivouacked with Rodes' brigade in the cornfield of Henry Piper. Relative quiet enveloped this sector of the line. Against orders, men killed, cooked, carved, and ate pigs stolen from Piper's stock. Satisfaction was hunger's only commander. Soldiers plucked and roasted corn left on the stalks to dry for feed.

Some of the command slept like newborns. Others wandered the ground, destined never again to know the peace of earthly sleep. Strains of "Bonnie Blue Flag" carried the music of home to ears of the restless.

Clouds gathered after midnight and a chilling sprinkle commenced. Bull reported for duty.

"Stokes," Teaseley said, smiling at the unflappable veteran, "where the hell you been? "Fill your belly and get some sleep."

Bull nodded as he eased the rifle strap from his shoulder. He saw a group of men standing and laughing near a pit fire. He removed his shoes, stretched and wiggled his reddened toes, and walked on the carpet of corn stalks and moistened earth toward the group of men.

"Mind if I have me a bite?" Bull asked as a matter of courtesy.

"He'p yourse'f, soldier," replied a stringy man no more than eighteen. "Plenty left."

"Coffee's hot," said another soldier. "Ain't had this kind of eatin' since Manassas."

Bull placed his rifle on the ground. He sliced a few strips of succulent pork and laid them on a warming plate he had picked off a dead officer at the second battle of Manassas. He poured the coffee, sniffed his steaming cup, and raised his eyebrows in contentment.

"Yep, it's real coffee, Yankee coffee. Well, border-state coffee, but it beats the hell out of mealy bugs and ragweed. Got a bit o' sugar here, if you'd like."

"Obliged," Bull said. "What's your name, soldier?"

"Pilchard. Avery Pilchard. Folks call me Spider."

"I can see why … Spider," Bull said, smiling as he studied the skeletal limbs of the underfed, over-marched lad. "Stokes is my name. Friends call me Bull. Where you from, Spider?"

Spider acknowledged with a smile, his teeth as white as moonlight. "Birmingham, Alabama," Spider said, his proud grip tightening around the barrel of his rifle. "We gawn see that elephant tomorrow, ain't we?"

"Reckon so," Bull replied, dipping a spoon into the sugar.

"Ain't never seen the elephant b'fore," Spider revealed, apprehension evident in his confession. "What's it like?"

Bull stared at the cloudy sky for a moment and turned to Spider.

"You'll do fine, Avery."

"I reckon I will, but ..."

"But what?" Bull sipped his coffee and folded a strip of pork between two hardtack crackers.

"Nerves, I s'pose. Sergeant says the whole Yankee army's right through them woods yonder, 'cross the creek."

"Lee's got his whole army ready to say 'hello'," Bull replied with a smile of reassurance, fully aware Lee's army could almost take a night swim in the Potomac. "Why don't you find yourself a spot and write your folks a letter?" Bull advised. "You got folks, ain't you?"

"Yep, got folks. Ain't got no paper. Pencil neither."

"Here, use mine," Bull said, reaching into his pocket and retrieving a piece of blank, creased paper and the stubbed pencil.

Spider took the paper and pencil from Bull's hand. "I can see why they call you Bull," Spider observed as the pit fire painted Bull's forearm and hand in shadow and light, revealing lean crevices of muscle and tendon and bone. "Give the pencil back to you directly, Bull."

Bull nodded and lay on a bed of stalks.

Just as Bull drifted to sleep, the familiar shrill of an artillery shell slapped him to consciousness. He scrambled for the cover of a supply wagon. The shell burst overhead, sending shards of sharp, white-hot metal hissing and howling amid the men, striking several. Stephen D. Lee's batteries replied in kind, and for a few moments the uneasy thought of a night-shielded Union assault gripped the soldiers.

The shell served its purpose. Relaxation became effort. Soldiers milled around, watchful for any movement in their front. Skirmishers were sent forward into the fields. Bull sat and rested his back against the supply wagon and pulled out his unfinished letter. He read silently:

Dearest Caroline,

It is 16 September, and we have crossed the Potomac River into Maryland. Plenty of beautiful countryside up here. Mountains, streams – makes me feel like I brought home with me. We hope to find more than enough food to fill our stomachs and shoes to cover our feet. Don't see a lot of smiling faces amongst the locals. Union loyalists, I reckon.

A fight like none other awaits us tomorrow. Marse Robert wants to take the fighting north. The men are excited and seem less nervous than usual, and even in the absence of provisions, laughter and song fill their mouths. The thought of injury or death looms as always, but something about this fight has the men distant of mind, almost spellbound, as if thrust into another world, filled with promise.

I write you, my dearest Caroline, to tell you to abandon all worry. I am in God's hands, and I have no fear of the enemy. If I am killed, know that I loved you as supremely as any man could and that my spirit will abide in the very air you breathe until we meet again.

Your Beloved Timothy, the "Bull"

Moment of Truth

Bull looked up and noticed the flurry of activity by the pit fire. Stretcher bearers stumbled to the site. He saw a man on his back, the light of the pit fire revealing his blood-soaked shirt. He walked over and stared at the man. Bull had witnessed this scenario with somber frequency.

Alive one minute, dead the next. The Lord giveth, and the Lord taketh away. Bull bent down and took the pencil gripped in the man's frozen hand. Paper, scribbled with the sentiment of frightened uncertainty and dotted with blood, rested on the man's chest.

Bull saw it coming.

"I'll get your letter home, Spider," Bull said.

Chapter 10

Last evening, the roads out of Sharpsburg choked with the traffic of human refugees. The moment was at hand. The question of a great battle in western Maryland no longer dominated the tables and hearths of homes and meeting places. The question asked was answered. The combatants had taken their positions, displacing families seeking the relative safety of Shepherdstown and Hagerstown and Boonsboro, the Antietam Iron Furnace, even Killiansburg Cave. The valley of the Antietam awaited the inevitable.

Rachael and Jacob had made the journey to and from Killing's Cave as often as they had traversed the length of Hog Trough Road. The cave was a frequent subject of Rachael's artwork and a cozy seclusion for the smitten teens. Now Rachael pressed the damp, dark road from the cave to Jacob's home. Claggett was alive!

Taking advantage of the swirl of pre-battle activity, Claggett had shuffled Bigun's family from the cave, unnoticed by everyone except Rachael. She needed to find Jacob, or his father, and tell the news.

Her darkness-adjusted eyes perceived the muted outline of the Hoffman home just ahead. She saw no lamplight. The night was deceptively quiet, crickets and tree frogs its only keepers. The land slept in its pretense of serenity.

Rachael made her way into the empty house. She kept a watchful guard, eyes shifting left to right, scanning the night for the unexpected, mindful of Claggett.

She knew the home and its contents as well as Jacob. She scraped a match along a cupboard and lit an oil lantern. The light cast distorted shadows as she moved from room to room. Objects seemed to swell and recede in the moving light like the waves of stormy seas. The floors dispensed groans with every step, as if hell itself were waking.

The bedrooms were empty, as expected. Household articles appeared undisturbed. Someone had eaten the food she prepared for Jacob and Bigun. Other items of food were missing; some foodstuffs were left alone. She placed the lantern on the floor, settled into a parlor chair, and decided to wait for Isaac's return.

The early morning calm exploded, stirring Rachael from her sleep. She gasped and opened her eyes.

"Jacob!"

Artillery pounded to the northeast. Rachael snapped to consciousness and raced to the porch. Hints of pastel yellows and grays painted their tentacles upon the eastern horizon. The great battle was on, and somewhere, Jacob was out there. Rachael grabbed a straw broom and swept with the vigor and haste of one expecting company.

Try as she may, Rachael's busyness did not quell the battle's rage and rancor. Volleys of musketry and salvos of artillery shattered the peace of the valley, as if someone had taken a sledgehammer to a pane of glass the size of Maryland.

Rachael stopped in her tracks as the faint pierce of a yipping yell plowed through her ears. The demonic shrill, blasted from existence almost as soon as it started, chilled her soul. She kept sweeping. For three hours she swept.

The battle's tree-muffled roar subsided, for now. Between bursts, Rachael detected the monotony of rattles and squeaks, distant at first but drawing steadily nearer. She continued sweeping, now but hollow waves of the broom, dodging clouds of dust shaken by the percussive vibrations of screaming shells. She noticed peculiar utterances growing louder and more frequent. Rachael cupped her ear.

She thought of the familiar high pitch of pig squeals and the mournful bellows of sunning cattle. *Strange*, she thought. She stepped onto the porch, cautious of stray projectiles, some of which had pecked the house earlier, and peeked down the road.

Wagons pulled by piteous horses streamed up Landing Road toward the house like a parade of the damned, their cargo of shot men stabbed further with each bounce of the wheels, arms and legs the dangles of stringless puppets.

Rachael gasped. The train of wagons had no end. Wounded men, their torn bodies awash in blood and dirt, wailed for water and their merciful release from life. The first of the battle's consequences arrived.

Orderlies hauled men to the bases of sycamores and oaks and grouped the wounded according to their probability of survival. Those able strained to lift arms high enough for notice, begging for relief from the agony swept upon them. Rachael set the broom against a porch post, along with her thoughts of Jacob and Isaac and Claggett, and waded, dazed, into the sea or anguish.

"Need water, ma'am, and linens, food, anything you got. Need this house," a Confederate orderly said with the calmness of Job and the experience of war. "Need you, too, ma'am. You men unhinge them doors and search the grounds for boards, logs, tables, anything to make places for the sawbones. We need hay and space for the wounded."

Moment of Truth

Rachael stared at the unthinkable. Her mouth opened, but no words followed.

Chapter 11

Late summer insects found a human feast in the fallow field. Jacob and Bigun dozed intermittently, neither of them mindful they might never again know the peace of sleep. Bigun slapped a mosquito on his arm and glimpsed the smear of first light. He nudged Jacob's shoulder.

"Jacob. *Jacob!*"

"Hmmm? What?" an agitated Jacob mumbled as he stirred and stretched his arms, his mind lost in blissful oblivion.

Then, like a mighty wind, the abruptness of reality rushed over him. His eyes opened. "Damn! Get *up*, Bigun! What time is it?"

"I's up, Jacob. Been up. I figger it to be, oh, five, six o'clock. Hear dat?"

Morning had lit the fuse. The tension was breached. Artillery salvos exploded a mile or two toward the northeast. The valley of the Antietam erupted. The battle was on.

"Dadgumit! I was havin' a fine dream that me an' Rachael were walkin' down the Hog Trough Road when lightnin' struck Ole Whooey's tree, just as we passed, scatterin' that ol' bird, an' *us* with 'im," Jacob said, a chuckle on his lips. "Rachael an' me fell to the ground and

… an' then a God-awful racket of thunder … *Come on, Bigun!*"

Jacob was determined to get a glimpse of the mighty Army of Northern Virginia, Lee's legions that had whipped Pope's beleaguered army just three weeks earlier at Manassas. He wondered if not following his pang to join this contemptible, yet refreshingly free band of Southern marauders, had been his lost opportunity for glory and adventure.

Jacob felt a tap on his back and turned. "Roswell?"

Isaac would have found Jacob and killed him before any Yankee bullet had the chance. He patted his pocket and felt the reassurance of his coin. He could buy adventure, he believed, but glory had to be earned.

Jacob and Bigun hastily gathered their belongings and cantered through the charcoal-gray field toward the sounds. They exited a patch of woods and stopped at the post-and-rail fence spanning the length of the Hagerstown Pike, a hundred yards south of a white square of a building the Dunkards called church. Jacob wondered if his Daddy and the Mummas had spent the night there.

The area teemed with rebel souls marching in line of battle through the treeless fields and countless others held in reserve sheltered by woods.

The Dunkard Church sat on ground donated for such by Samuel Mumma. The structure looked like a whitewashed box with a roof. No steeple. No pretension. No immodesty.

The church was built on a rise of ground at the intersection of the Hagerstown Pike and the Smoketown Road. It was an unassuming feature bordered on the east by fields of farmers' labor and on the west and north by a few acres of woods. This ordinary spot of antiwar holiness soon would quake within the grasp of mighty armies, desperate individual struggles for survival and conquest.

Shrouded by the mist, Jacob grabbed a rail and pulled atop the fence to gain a clearer view of morning and the mix of human emotion. Electricity filled the air. Cannon and caissons rumbled up the pike and across fields, spitting dirt and rocks in their wake and scattering groups of startled stragglers before them. A battery of Rebel artillery, facing north, lined a ridge in Mumma's field a hundred yards east of the church. These were the guns of S.D. Lee, the wheels of their 12-pounder Howitzers leaping off the ground with each thunderous belch of iron and flame.

Wow! Jacob thought, pressing his palms against his ears.

Silhouettes of horses swept over the roll of fields, riders urging their mounts with shouts of "Heeyah!" and the frenzied lashings of the reigns. Lines of smoke from countless breakfast fires, abandoned to burn themselves out, drifted straight into the air and dissipated above the trees into a blanket of haze. A mass of Confederates double-quicked past Jacob as he climbed over the fence and stumbled, dazed, onto the Hagerstown Pike.

Jacob and Bigun stared in awe at this birth of an inferno, a scene of the surreal pulled straight from the worst nightmare.

The battle exploded before them. North of the church, in David Miller's corn, volleys of musketry crashed back and forth, sweeping lives away like dirt off a floor.

Artillery shells exploded over the heads of men, raining death down with randomness and reason, understood only by God.

Bullets by the thousands pinged and thudded, buzzed and crunched, an incessant symphony of madness. Bodies jerked as if attached to the strings of puppeteers, lifeblood spewing from ghastly holes. Men shouted, screamed, defiant as long as life allowed.

Moment of Truth

Soldiers did not look like soldiers, not as Jacob had imagined soldiers might look going into battle. These were energetic, confident, eager men ready to accomplish their duty and move on. Their experienced steps were quick to the drummer's tap-tap-tap. Their chins were high, eyes forward, resolve firm. Rifles rested erect against their right shoulders. Officers gripped sabers, raised high and mirror-clean. Pockets of men counted time singing "Yellow Rose of Texas". Laughter spilled from the mouths of these tanned, leathered men. Expletives and oaths rolled off tongues like water from a downspout.

These men marching in front of Jacob and Bigun, led by Colonel William Wofford, had only glory to lose, their lives all but sacrificed the moment they mustered in. Their colors boldly announced the single white star of the Texas Brigade, a blending of troops from Texas, Georgia and South Carolina. Red banners of the Southern Cross snapped the brigade's optimism to the beat of the breeze.

Ahead, up the Pike and beyond the church, the corn of David Miller heaved with relentless explosions and shouts, bullets and blood, a perfect firestorm of angst and bitterness. Moans followed the clatter of angry musketry, a hellish anthem to the rhythms of death.

Men simply disappeared in the face of canister, sheets of lead scything through what corn remained and cutting to shreds all flesh in its path. Eyes, moments earlier seething with a lust to kill, lay frozen in their moment of truth, not a speck of enmity amid their dilation.

The quest for glory, for adventure, ended in the anonymity of somebody's cornfield far from everybody's home. Boys from Georgia, Mississippi, Louisiana, and Texas, Pennsylvania, New York, Wisconsin and Rhode Island fell, their bodies slammed to the ground in exclamation, their futures silenced.

The screams and wails of desperate wounded, many trampled by the charges and counter-charges, begged for relief, for the only hope of glory left–death. The ground itself seemed to writhe.

"Come on, Bigun," shouted Jacob, "this way!"

Jacob pulled on Bigun's shirt, trying to shake the big man free from his trance of shock. Remnants of regiments and walking wounded streamed rearward to the safety of the trees behind the church, their proud colors shell-torn and bullet-riddled, clawed and ripped by the blue lions.

"Hey, boy, take you up a rifle and come on!" shouted a laughing voice in a throng of voices. Others chuckled at the unlikely notion.

A black man and a skinny white boy, wandering around like dazed kids at a carnival, they thought. Front-row seat.

Jacob looked forward and behind, not certain he was the target of the jest but wishing to God he was not.

"Me?" he asked, feigning surprise.

"No, I was talkin' to that fencepost beside you!"

Soldiers, fresh from the face of the fight, laughed in spite of the carnage, perhaps because of it.

Jacob smiled and glanced at Bigun.

"I'm–I'm only fifteen," Jacob explained.

"See that lad over there?" a soldier asked Jacob, pointing to the corner of the Dunkard Church. "He claims he's sixteen, but shit, we all know he's twelve, maybe eleven. Hell, his musket's taller than he is!"

Indeed, the boy was like an ear of corn to a cornstalk, and Jacob wondered how he handled the unwieldy weapon.

"Damn good shot, he is. *Damn* good. Sharpshooter with Ripley's command. He can handle a nine-pound musket better'n most grown men. Cain't afford to send 'im out in this melee, not right now. Too damn valu'ble. He can plug an acorn from a squirrel's mouth at two hundred paces.

"How old are *you?*" Jacob asked.

"Just turned nineteen, an' I'm gawn go kill me some Yankees. Where'd you git this here nigger?"

"He ain't no … *that!* He's a *man*, just like you an' me."

"Maybe like you, he is, but not like me," the soldier replied, scanning Bigun head to toe. "Freed man or slave?"

Jacob looked with shame at Bigun. "Freed," Jacob lied.

"Then git him a rifle, too. We need bodies! All blood's the same color," the soldier shouted as he scampered up the Pike to catch up with his unit.

"You're exactly where I want to be," uttered Jacob.

"What the hell are you talkin' about?" another passing soldier asked in amazement, forgetting that he, too, once was filled with this same naiveté.

"I'm talkin' about you're a Confederate soldier fightin' with the Robert E. Lee. Don't that mean somethin' to you?"

The young soldier laughed. "What's your name, buck?"

"Jacob Hoffman. An' yours?"

"Rushin. Sergeant T.J. Rushin, 12th Georgia."

Sergeant Rushin stood six feet-four inches, hair like wheat and eyes of hazel. His left arm just above the elbow was bandaged and bloodied. Jacob stared at the wound and suspected a bullet had done this work but dared not venture into so private an issue. This was a man headed toward the fray, not away from it.

"This?" Rushin said, touching his elbow and sensing Jacob's curiosity. "Hell, boy, this ain't nothin'. I got hurt worse plowin' with Sister Sara back home. Damn mule would kick a man for *thinkin'!* Yanks gawn have to do a hell of a lot better'n this if they want *me* out of the fight."

"What's the T.J. stand for," Jacob pried.

"Thomas Jefferson, but it's a damn might easier to just call me T.J.–or, in your case, 'sir'."

"Yes, sir."

"Aw, hell, boy, I'm just *joshin'* you. Now, you asked me if bein' a Confederate soldier fightin' with the Robert E. Lee meant somethin'. Depends."

"On what?"

"On if I get to sit in the tent with 'im whilst these boys fight."

Jacob stared speechless.

"See that officer over yonder standin' next to the 12-pounder?" he asked, pointing to Captain William Parker barking orders and pacing the battery poised on the low ridge across the pike from the Dunkard Church.

Jacob didn't know a 12-pounder from a siege mortar but figured the officer to whom T.J. referred must be the man gesturing in every direction.

"I see 'im."

"Got a wife at home pregnant with a baby he'll prob'ly never see. Little Mac's got most of his boys over on the other side of the Antietam. What you see up yonder's just a taste. They gawn give us all we care to take," said Rushin as he shifted his musket strap to a less worn part of his shoulder. "A whole mess of us seen their last sunrise this mornin'. Some are gone; some'll be gone before the sun sets. I'd give my sweet mother to be in your shoes now. I spect the Cap'n would too."

"Where you from, Sergeant Rushin?" Jacob asked.

"A slice of heaven in South Georgia called Buena Vista," Rushin replied. "Reckon you don't know where that is."

"Reckon I don't," Jacob said, filled with wonder at what a land Georgia must be.

"It don't matter. Home's wherever I can find me some ripe roastin' ears fer my belly an' a pillow of straw fer my head. I got me a little lady down there, eighteen years old and ready, if you know what I mean. Course, I don't reckon you *do* know what I mean, do you, boy?"

Jacob thought about Rachael. "Oh yeah. I got me a good idea what you're talkin' about, T.J.," he said, a grin spreading across his face.

Rushin chuckled as he put fire to his pipe and sucked. Smoke snaked out his mouth. "She's worth dodgin' bullets fer, if I can just figure me out a way. Right now, we gotta keep these Yankees from comin' down south."

"By headin' north?" Jacob asked.

"Gotta git by these boys first, I reckon. Lee's tryin' to force Lincoln to sue fer peace. All we need is one more like Manassas, an' us between the Yanks and Washington, an' England might just be willin' to run the blockade fer cotton. We was kinda hopin' Little Mac might just step aside so's we could put a quick end to this war. Reckon he's got other ideas."

"I reckon," Jacob replied, his eyes afar with fascination and glazed with befuddlement by the political complexities. "Lookin' like a helluva fight."

Sergeant Rushin gazed at the smoke of battle.

"Yeah," he said softly, resignation in his voice.

Rushin took another suck on his pipe and blew the smoke with a sigh.

"Don'chu wanna kill Yankees?" Jacob asked.

"Hell, yeah, I wanna kill 'em! I wanna kill 'em because I know they want to kill *me!* Trouble with battle ain't the killin'. It's the noise. Damn noise. Racket fills your ears, like somebody smacked you upside the head with a snowball, snowball after snowball, bullets whistlin' by, shells screamin' through the air." Rushin paused, eyes fixed on the translucent portal of his future. "Men shoutin', dying.

"The noise I can take, I reckon, the more I think about it. It's the noise I *cain't* hear that scares me. You never hear the bullet that's meant for you. It'll come out the barrel of a rifle held by a man you ain't never met, ain't got no personal quarrel with. It'll cut the air like lightnin', a beeline for your body. But you don't hear it. Bullet hits you before the sound does."

The wounded and the expended streamed rearward.

"I just hope my bullet kills me right off. I don't want to linger on the field gut-shot or limb-shattered, unable to move, no water, no relief, no hope. If I'm meant to die in this war, this battle, I want to die *right off*," Rushin said with a sweep of his arms. "I don't want to be shot by some half-assed Yankee who closes his eyes every time he pulls the trigger."

Jacob said nothing; his words felt puny.

"Move 'em out, Sergeant!" a captain yelled.

"Sir! Well," Rushin said, his voice firm with the acceptance of his fate, "Time to see the elephant. Again."

"See *what?*" Jacob asked.

"We're headin' into that jungle yonder, takin' our boys to victory. Got a hankerin' fer glory? Gitchu a rifle an' a cartridge box. Git one fer your friend, too. Plenty of glory to go around. Plenty of rifles stacked over yonder. Those men won't be needin' 'em, but my boys sure as hell need y'all."

Jacob's eyes spanned the open fields as he walked with Rushin. Columns of men marched north on the Hagerstown Pike. Others, awaiting orders, lingered in the woods behind the church.

Jacob stopped as he heard shouts of "Into battery!" Platoons of guns unlimbered and caissons of ammunition chests deployed. No more were the late summer socials that filled the fields of Sharpsburg and the valley of the Antietam Creek in early autumn. Hundreds of holed shoes, feet covered with little more than dirt and blood, shuffled northward, their sound silenced by the greater calamity.

"Can I get me a couple of them muskets stacked over there?" Jacob asked a soldier slow to respond to officers' commands. "Pay for 'em, that is." Jacob patted his pocket. He did not intend to comply with Sergeant Rushin's plea for men.

"*Pay* fer 'em?" Rushin shouted, overhearing Jacob's selfish request. "Boy, the only tender we'll take for them rifles is your service. This ain't no general store. If you want to take up a rifle, it comes with an elephant. Now get to it an' leave my men be!"

What's he talkin' about, an elephant? Jacob thought, his mind set on confiscating a Springfield and skedaddling to a world he believed safe.

The soldier, skin grimed with black powder thick around his mouth, hair curled and clingy with sweat, gathered his cartridge box and rifle and fell into rank with the rest of the slim body of men. The unit, depleted further by the morning's first round of service, had taken losses in the prior weeks at Second Manassas and South Mountain.

He tossed his haversack onto the stack of others. Such would only hinder him now. He needed nothing else save the letter and photograph from home tucked inside the sweatband of his hat. A bit of Irish luck and the favor of God, should he be so graced, sweetened his chances. He marched in a right oblique maneuver across Mumma's grass, just south of the Smoketown Road and east of the Hagerstown Pike. He was numb to his chances of surviving a second round.

"Soldier?" Jacob started.

"Cain't talk now," the soldier blurted, his words more prophetic than he imagined.

"Come on, Bigun!" Jacob said as he trotted toward the stack of arms.

"Jacob, you ain't about to do what I thinks you 'bout to do, is you?"

"Bigun, I'm just gawn get me a rifle, a *Yankee* rifle, one of them Springfields! An' I get to keep my five dollar gold! Cain't beat *that* at the cockfights! Don't you want one of those rifles?"

"But dem rifles is fo' *fightin'*. You ain't gawn fight, is you?"

"I ain't gawn fight. Come on, Bigun!"

"A black man, a slave, behind Rebel lines, with a weapon? Jacob, I might as well draw me a red bullseye on dis white shirt."

"Come *on*, Bigun! They're payin' about as much attention to us as a glass of water in a saloon."

Jacob neared the glistening rifles, a shambled stack behind the church.

Mayhem dominated the area a few hundred yards north of the church and toward a patch of woods across from what yesterday was farmer Miller's field of harvest-ready corn. Solid shot plowed the soil, digging long furrows, bouncing and ripping torsos from men. The field held a harvest of a different sort today.

Jacob watched the fight in full view of a division of Yankee troops forming on a low rise in Mummas field across the road from the church. Stray bullets pattered the walls of the church, each strike sending a small explosion of dust and paint into the air. The thought did not occur to Jacob that one of those strays might be lethal or that his standup posture presented an irresistible target for an army target-hungry.

"Look, Bigun! Yankee Springfields! Every dadgum one of 'em." Jacob's face shined like a Christmas tree.

Jacob made a beeline for the bounty when a blue form caught his eye. A Yankee lay on his back, one knee bent, his lifeless body perforated with bullets. Jacob stared, the man's eyes and mouth wide-open, utter shock frozen into his glare. Flies appeared and vanished around the

Yankee's mouth, the buzzing a rising and receding constant. The soldier held a musket, a Springfield, in his stiff grasp, as if it were a child's bedtime toy. Jacob gently wrenched the rifle from the man's curled fingers. He wiped the pliable blood from the stock and barrel. He sighed and stared at the prize, blood freed and ownership duly transferred. He picked up the cartridge box and looked once more at the man.

Bigun stooped, paused, then reached and snapped up one of the Springfields from the stack.

Both walked a quick pace south on the Hagerstown Pike, away from the action northward.

"Did you see that poor bastard back there?" Jacob asked.

"I seen 'im. He had at least five new holes in him. A frightful sight."

"I'm talkin' about that look in his eye, his face. Wonder what he felt, what he thought, when he was hit," Jacob pondered.

"Dem eyes looked like he realized he'd walked into somethin' he had no chance of gettin' away from, like Satan's parlor," Bigun observed. "Don't reckon he had a chance to feel much of nothin'."

"Okay you two, let's go, let's move it! Now!" shouted a Confederate, his sleeves adorned with chevrons.

"Hey, we ain't–"

"Boy, I don't repeat myself. Don't make me shoot you and the darkie right here in this road. Now git on over there, in that road yonder, other side of that corn!" the soldier shouted, pointing toward Hog Trough Road.

Jacob and Bigun obeyed. They trotted through Piper's orchard and corn toward the road. They saw a battery of rebel guns deploying to their left. Up ahead, through Piper's corn, they saw a mass of men and arms squirming within the confines of a sunken road.

"Jesus, my *Jesus!*" Jacob said, gasping. "Hog Trough!"

"Jacob, you don't reckon dey's about to put us in dis fight, do you? Don't dey know we ain't soldiers?"

"I reckon they know *you* ain't no soldier, Bigun, but they need bodies, an' for that you're as guilty as me. I guess we found our hideaway."

"It done found us," Bigun said.

Chapter 12

"Right here, boys!" instructed a sergeant from the Sixth Alabama. "Squeeze in right here, and ready those weapons."

"But we ain't soldiers!" Jacob protested.

"You are now. What Lee don't know won't hurt 'im."

"But sergeant–"

"Look here boy," the sergeant said, pointing his Colt at Jacob's face, "this ain't no debate. Gitchur ass in that line and ready your weapon."

Jacob looked at his weapon, its stewardship bequeathed to him minutes earlier by the passing of a man known only to God.

Soldiers glanced back at the approach of Jacob and Bigun. They peered at Bigun, an armed black man, as he slumped to his knees and propped his Springfield against the fence-rail breastwork.

"Damn fine rifle fer a Negro," noted a private.

"Here, you take it," Bigun replied, indifferent to the white man's fight. "I jus' as soon walk down dat road an' nevuh look back."

"Walk down that road an' never look back? Boy, that's *suicide!* You'll end up dead in that corn or shackled in a wagon bound fer South Carolina. No, you best stay here an' defend yourself. Ain't a man in this line got anything agin a Negro fightin' alongside us. This is your ticket to freedom, boy."

"I's free now, on my way to Philadelphia."

The soldier looked at Jacob. "This nigger yours?"

"It's like he told you; he's free."

"I don't know about free, but I do know about black," the private preached, "and there's plenty of scruff out there willin' to take you as theirs or kill you where you stand. I know your chances are better if we see you shootin' them Yanks a-comin'. You know how to fire that weapon, boy?"

"I learned the musket long b'fo you was a pup. I can take the balls off a bee wit' a rock," Bigun boasted. "I can *sho'* knock somethin' down with dis."

Jacob smiled, proud of Bigun's stand amid a sea of white.

The private grinned with uneasiness, mindful the enemy might be among him.

"Well, see to it … soldier."

Hog Trough Road was not so much a road as it was a wagon-worn passage, in spots four feet below the bordering ground of surrounding fields. Etched into the earth over three generations, the lane was a Sharpsburg bypass, spurring east from the Hagerstown Pike, then southeast to a zigzagged rendezvous with Piper's Lane and the Boonsboro Road. Post-and-rail fences, splintered by age and broken with neglect, lined the lengths of both embankments.

The morning awoke in a shroud of clouds and to the thunder of battle. Hog Trough Road hung suspended under heaven and tethered above hell, destiny awaiting its turn. The center of Lee's line stretched along a thousand yards of the road's slopes and dismantled fences. Its chasm seemed scratched into the bucolic landscape like a mass grave filled with the living.

Wayward rabbits were crushed under the weight of waiting humans. Anxious, shouting men lay wagers for the privilege of bayoneting field mice. Men exchanged frantic, fantastic bets in card games believed their last. Decks of cards dotted the ground as others forsook their sinful ways and grasped their last measure of repentance. The fury of the fight that came in early morning was no stranger to these men. Nor was the fury to come.

South of Hog Trough Road was Henry Piper's cornfield, Ole Whooey's domain, stalks of tan and green swaying their indifference in the morning breeze. The north side of the road bordered an expanse of grass and corn extending well beyond the farms of Mumma and Roulette. The undulation of the ground, its dips and rises, swales and knolls, offered for a precious moment the relief of cover and the realization of the horror that waited atop each crest.

The fight near Sharpsburg was barely two hours old and already the serene fields a mile north of town were choked with the debris and blood of unprecedented violence. Union General George Greene's Second Division, Twelfth Corps, had penetrated Confederate lines into the woods surrounding the Dunkard Church west of the Hagerstown Pike. This attack, characteristic of all Union thrusts of the morning, was isolated and unsupported, Georgians and Virginians pushing Greene's men back across the Hagerstown Pike.

Then came General John Sedgwick's turn. Sedgwick's Second Corps division, line after blue line of infantry, trod over the open ground north of Smoketown Road. The Union objective, the whitewashed speck of a church set against the dark green of woods, was the same as it had been since the battle's first shot.

Confederate divisions commanded by McLaws and Walker, concealed in the woods behind the church, turned Sedgwick's left flank, pouring coordinated volleys of musketry into the Yankees' front, left, and rear. Panicked soldiers streamed north and east, mindless of the dead and wounded comrades over which they trampled and the blood through which they splashed.

The battle raged in the Dunkard Church sector for two hours. The Rebels holding Lee's center in the Hog Trough Road, just south of the church, sat and listened with growing apprehension as the storm of battle swirled to a crescendo a half-mile to their north. One way or another, their turn was coming.

The savage pop of musketry and intermittent screams of artillery shells died down, indications the battle near the church had spent its energy and was shifting elsewhere. Greene and Sedgwick repulsed, the Rebel left flank held.

The sickening ooze of blood replaced the lush green of corn and grass. Since the break of light, fire had fallen from the sun and ascended from hell, squeezing the battlefield and its occupants in its merciless inferno of carnage. Thousands of bodies, stilled and writhing, dotted the countryside. The day, and the killing, had just begun.

A macabre lull settled over the northern end of the battlefield. Countless wounded, trapped in the mangle of their gore and sprawled across the crimson fields and fences and trees and bramble, like the scattered debris of a tornado, let loose a sickening cacophony of agony, displacing the roar of cannon and the spin of bullets. The fearless became the helpless.

McClellan sent General William French, commander of the Second Corps's third division, splashing across the Antietam Creek to support the Union left flank at the woods near the church. Instead, unable to find Sedgwick's shattered, scattered division through the smoke-draped landscape, French's command drifted left oblique southwestwardly, in the direction of Lee's center at the Hog Trough Road.

Confederate shells shrieked overhead ripping branches from trees, showering anxious men with leaves and branches and giving notice the elephant waited just ahead. Inexperienced regiments from obscure villages in Pennsylvania, New York, Ohio, Delaware, and Maryland pressed forward over farmer Roulette's land and around his farmhouse, disturbing stacked crates of honeybees and tasting their first sting of battle.

More Rebels, under the division command of Daniel Harvey Hill, spilled into Hog Trough Road in answer to the new Yankee threat, filling every inch of the thousand-yard, boomerang-shaped span.

Desperation replaced the ephemeral swagger of success earned moments earlier from having ambushed Sedgwick's thrust into the woods north and west of the Dunkard Church.

Lee's left flank, many of its soldiers borrowed from other parts of the line, had held against McClellan's staccato, broken advances of the early morning. McClellan's predictable caution was Lee's salvation, allowing Lee to focus resources where needed in lieu of defending an entire line of battle against a concentrated assault.

As if prepared by the gods of war, Hog Trough Road served a position advantageous for its Confederate possessors. The protection provided by terrain and fence; the security of unbroken numbers; the strength of leadership; the courage of hardened flesh and blood; a sense of invulnerability earned from a summer of fighting; all of this was immutable in the minds of Southern soldiers searching for a foothold in the psychology of battle.

Yet, beneath the pretense of relative advantage, reality lurked, stark in its punch of truth. The time was now. Nowhere to run. Nowhere to advance. Nowhere to hide. Reserves were spent and scarce. The stand for the Confederacy was here in Hog Trough Road. Turn the enemy or die in the attempt. Ole Whooey clung to his branch and watched the strange dance, head tilted.

Thousands of memories for hundreds of lives melded into a mighty weld of anticipation at this single brink of eternity.

The last breath of summer rustled across the valley, a cooling respite from the sizzle of the September sun. The sky teased, exchanging its intermittent ripples of heat with the occasional relief of the billow of clouds. Rain might fall; it might not; either way, lightning and thunder were certainties.

Rifles rested on fence rails, pointed toward an enemy unseen but no less present. Orders barked. Men obeyed. Flags snapped. Runners carried messages. Flies buzzed. Sweat rolled. Eyes squinted. Stomachs growled; for some, they heaved. Grasshoppers sprang in all directions tending to their instincts for survival. Homes beckoned, and hearts sank with the suddenness of truth, like the plunge off a cliff.

Men in regiments from Alabama and North Carolina and remnants of Colquitt's Georgia brigade, all under the command of Generals Rodes and Anderson, occupied the rutted stretch. To take Sharpsburg, McClellan's Yankees had to pierce Lee's center, the attempts of the early morning on Lee's left dismal failures. McClellan had to take Hog Trough Road. Ole Whooey peered, still and unblinking, an ignorant sage to the folly unfolding.

Jacob yanked the paper tip off the cartridge with his teeth, bits of black powder scattering through the air and into his mouth. He spat the bitter grains from his tongue, its taste of sulfur as repulsive as week-old coffee. He shoved the remaining propellant down the barrel, his eyes fixed upon the crest of a low ridge seventy-five yards in front. He hadn't the relief of shade. No one did. He wiped away ranks of sweat assaulting his skin wherever gravity took them. He looked right and left, then right again.

Hundreds of human lives, elbow upon elbow, crouched behind fence rails, mouthed words of prayer for deliverance. Butterflies, bees, and grasshoppers fluttered, buzzed, and jumped from the green of the sloping field facing the soldiers, as if nothing extraordinary were happening, like a breath of contradiction.

Some men stared into space, forming a mind's-eye image of the do-or-die fight to come. Others craned peeks in the direction of the invisible enemy.

Some laughed to conceal their fear.

Some lounged, hats over eyes, awaiting orders they had heard before, the whole experience the drudgery of repetition.

Some sang songs of home.

Some stole bites of plundered hardtack. Some drank the last from their canteens, tossing the obtrusive vessels aside.

Some lit pipes and sucked fires that never caught.

Some shouted obscenities.

Some penned hastened letters to loved ones and stuffed the scribblings into pockets.

Others prayed without ceasing for lives spared.

All were scared, though none admitted it.

A few soldiers scattered to take up positions as skirmishers along the ridgeline.

Near the point in the line where Hog Trough Road intersected Roulette's lane–the apex of the boomerang–a man of the 2nd North Carolina rested his rifle, raised his head, and let loose.

"Whenever I turn to view the place, the tears doth fall and blind me;

"When I think of the charming grace, of the girl I left behind me.

"My mind her image full retains; whether asleep or awakened;

"I hope to see my jewel again; for her my heart is breaking."

Soldiers looked toward the source of the melody. A short, vacuous silence gripped the line, followed piecemeal by others joining the singing of the somber, solemn song. Soon, the entire line sounded the mournful words. Men mouthed the tune with one eye toward home, unable to spill the sounds without pouring their tears, resigned that fate might well give them a new home.

Jacob, ignorant of the song and its meaning, dropped the .58-caliber projectile down the muzzle of his U.S. Springfield, a possession prized in the steady hands of a Confederate, taken from the frozen hands of a swollen Yankee at the woods near the Dunkard Church. He stuffed ball and powder home, removed the ramrod and plunged it within quick reach into the rain-softened embankment, an act born more of common sense than experience. Now the wait.

"Bigun, you load up?" Jacob asked.

"What fo'? To kill the ones come to liberate me? I'm sittin' on the wrong side of dis fight, Jacob."

"Bigun, them soldiers ain't come to liberate *nobody!* Them soldiers are here because somebody convinced 'em of the glory and adventure of war, same as Roswell. And the meals, the uniform, a rifle, an' thirteen dollars a month. Their officers are here because Lee's here. Ain't no politicians here, least not the ones who'll take a bullet. You think those men give a rat's ass about your freedom?"

"Frederick Douglass gives a rat's ass. John Brown give a rat's ass. Thas all I needs to know."

"Bigun, if you *don't* fight, if you walk away, *these* soldiers are liable to put a bullet in your skull, or worse, your back," Jacob said, waving his hand in reference to the Confederates in the road. "You wanna be shot in the back?"

Bigun thought a moment. "Rock an' a hard place," he answered.

"Rock an' a hard place," Jacob acknowledged.

"You here 'cause you wawna be?" Bigun asked.

"Not at first," Jacob answered after some thought. "All I wanted was a rifle an' some distance 'tween us an' Claggett. But what I seen yesterday in Sharpsburg an' back yonder at the church, well, it set me to thinkin'."

"'Bout what?"

"'Bout these rebs. They look like hell's stepchildren, but they got a spark in their eyes I ain't seen on any Yankee."

"When has you seen a Yankee's eyes 'cept a dead one?" Bigun asked, propping his head against a fence rail.

"Rachael said these rebs ain't out-spirited. She's right. I bet nary a one of these men has even *seen* a slave, much less *owned* one. They're jus' defendin' their homes, same as you an' me an' anybody else."

"By comin' up here, up north?"

"I reckon they got a right to push Lincoln's army out of their country."

"*Their* country? Sounds to me like you's had a change of heart, Jacob."

"Not about slavery, Bigun. I loathe it more than ever, an' I know you deserve to be as free as any white man."

"But, Jacob, if de South wins—"

"I know, Bigun, I know. It don't make no sense to me, neither. Maybe I'm here because of Roswell. Maybe I'm here for Rachael. Maybe it's because Hog Trough is *our* road, mine an' Rachael's. Shit, maybe I'm here 'cause

128

Daddy don't want me here, who knows. Maybe I'm just afraid to turn tail, afraid that sergeant will shoot me. All I know is I'm here, an' I believe God had somethin' to do with that."

"God?" Bigun stared at Jacob. He shook his head and pulled the hammer on his musket to half-cock.

Veteran soldiers of Lee's army peered across the expanse of ground. The growing tension exacerbated personal discomforts of diarrhea, toothaches, hunger, mosquito bites, and the unquenchable longing to be somewhere else.

Sweat mixed with the black of powder and the filth of soldiering and gave at once to the line of men a singular appearance of a great scaled serpent, the red of battle flags writhing in the wind like festering wounds, the glint of steel dancing to the cadence of twenty-five hundred pulses.

Isolated pools of perspiration formed in the crevices of foreheads, which on occasion spilled forth, pushed by floods of the memories of home.

Bare feet, bruised, blistered, and cut, had now a chance for rest. Most of these men, mere boys three Christmases ago, were husbands; daddies; farmers; craftsmen and proprietors busy taming their corners of the world and scantly attentive to the orations of men bent on forging history and carving a new country. Men wiggled their contorted toes in the cool soil, mindless of this tiny luxury.

Now they were veterans, survivors of a war bellowed in the beginning to be a ninety-day distraction, a glorious excursion to faraway places. Home by August, they were promised. That was a year ago. Then, last April, the war for Southern independence took an ugly turn at Shiloh. All hope for a quick end dissolved.

Since their muster, they had experienced the bloodlettings at First and Second Manassas and the Seven Days and South Mountain, and now Sharpsburg. These were grizzled rebels bearing arms against a teetering union, fighting more because "they're down here" than for any pretense of forming a nation of their own, as the politicians saw fit to do, as their kin had done nearly a century prior. The desire to hold another man as chattel seemed a laughable reason to kill one another, especially to these men whose calloused hands themselves were now the property of the Confederacy.

"Them Yanks ain't gawn take this road!" Jacob shouted, turning his head side to side as he spoke, standing in defiance. "*Look* at this place! Jesus *hisself* couldn't take this road!"

"Git down, dumbass!" said a soldier. "Them Yankees are about to give us the devil, but first they gawn give you *hell!*"

"Jesus hisse'f ain't *got* to take this road," replied a whiskered soldier crouched next to Jacob. "Tha's what He's got them Irish fellers fer," he said, pointing northward and referring to General Thomas Meagher's Irish Brigade. "Them boys'll wade through hell an' drag a bit of it with 'em."

"Yeah. Well. Bring them Irish on is all I got to say," demanded the sinewy Jacob, eager to engage his newfound enemy, as he spat specks of gunpowder to the ground. "It don't matter a damn who comes! A Hoffman can kick an Irish just as easy."

The man chuckled at Jacob's boastful ignorance.

"Careful, boy. We got some Irish lads among us who just as soon put a bullet in you as shoot a Yankee. Anyway, they'll be on soon enough, boy. Best you have a little talk with your Jesus, make your peace, scrawl your name on a piece of paper an' shove it in your pocket. An' for God's sake putchur damn *head* down lest you attract the twitchin's of a nervous Yankee finger!"

"Make my *peace?* I got my *peace* in the barrel of this here rifle," Jacob declared, ducking for a moment to ground level and patting the barrel like a pet hound, "an' I intend on givin' them Yanks a little taste of … peace."

Bigun glared at Jacob, astonished with his abrupt bravado.

Jacob seemed fearless because he had never known fear. Not real fear. Not the sort of fear that gripped a man's mind like the jaws of a grizzly around the head of a trout. Not the sort of fear that crept into a man's soul, like rot into a fruit, unyielding in its determination, unforgiving in its finality.

His naiveté was his best friend—and his worst enemy. His mind's inability to grasp the coming killing was a measure of innocence long ago ripped from the veterans that filled Hog Trough Road. A collision loomed between the brutality of battle and the fantasy of youth, a convergence of divergent wills, a pivotal struggle between his delusions of immortality and the deadening fury of war.

Colonel Charles Tew, 2nd North Carolina, paced the line and gazed across the rolling fields to his front, anger and determination in the slits of his eyes, the look of a fear aged and pounded, like molten iron, into a defiant respect for his foe. Death stared back.

Colonel John Gordon commanded the 6th Alabama regiment, holders of the apex of Hog Tough Road. His men occupied the road to the immediate left of Tew's North Carolinians. Gordon turned to see a general, right arm in a sling, canter with his aides to a dirt-slung stop a few paces to the rear of the line. The two saluted and exchanged pleasantries.

Jacob noticed the meeting, particularly the austerity of their expressions. Jacob's companion rolled onto his side and propped his right leg and rifle against a fence rail and took up a strip of rye between his teeth.

"Officers and politicians," he observed, the blade of grass bobbing between his lips like a wagging finger. "We're better off without 'em."

Moment of Truth

The soldiers on this day, at this moment, understood the gravity of their predicament and were less disposed to dispense with the spontaneity of cheers for their beloved commander. The matter of sudden death far from home held more sway. A personal visit to the front lines by the Commander of the Army of Northern Virginia meant one thing only–desperation. Men sat on the road's slope, heads rested on hands pressed against the muzzles of rifle barrels. Their eyes stared at nothing. Their minds pondered everything.

"Boy, that there's Marse Robert and General Daniel Harvey Hill," the man said to Jacob.

"Robert E. *Lee*?" Jacob asked in full surprise. *The* Robert E. Lee?" Jacob asked again as if confirming the Second Coming.

"Well, don't go wetchur britches, boy! He's a damn good general, but he *ain't* the Almighty," the man said, not once blinking his eyes as he spat bits of rye grass. "He pisses on the ground, same as the rest of us."

"I'll be damned!" Jacob said. "I'll be *God-damned!* Robert E. Lee himself."

Soldiers strained to hear their commander's words. Lee gazed through binoculars toward the north and northeast.

"Hold this line, Colonel. Hold it at all peril, and do not let it go," Lee said as he handed the binoculars to his adjutant.

Lee's mount shuffled and danced, sensing with impatience the serpent approaching beyond the ridge. Indeed, the snake was at its hooves.

"We will *stay* here until the sun goes down or victory is *won!*" Colonel Gordon promised with a voice that growled like a cornered animal.

"God go with you, Colonel," Lee replied with a salute.

Those who heard Gordon's pledge knew well it was
a metaphor for death, though perhaps the words were not
intended as such. These men of Southern stock were
resolute in their determination to repulse the Union storm
approaching. The soldiers knew they had honor going in;
the task now was to hold on to honor going out. Most
preferred the plunge into the uncertainty of battle than the
surrender of honor. These men, save for Jacob, had seen
mayhem enough to render their conscience as numb as bare
skin in a January blow. A cold acceptance enveloped their
spirit.

"Heh, heh, ain't I heard *that* a hunnerd times b'fore!
I give Gordon his due, though. He's a man among officers
and fights as good as any soldier I ever seen. This your
first fight, boy?" asked the man, swatting a sweat bee.

"*No!*" lied Jacob. "What I mean is … it ain't like I
don't know what to do! My daddy taught me how to shoot
two, maybe three, rounds a minute. Let's see Billy top
that."

"*Billy?* Where's your respect, boy?" the man said
with a laugh. "That's about what I thought, two rounds a
minute. What's your name, anyhow?"

"Maybe *three!* Jacob Hoffman. How 'bout you?"

"Bull Stokes. First off, boy, you better hope them
Yankees don't pick this stretch right off to bring their
shootin'. See where this road bends right over there? From
where you an' me are sittin' to right over yonder on the
other side of that bend is the 6th Alabama. That's where
they'll push the issue, if not sooner, then later. When you
see whachur in for, you might just find yourself skedaddlin'
right up that bank," Bull said, gesturing with his head to the
cornfield behind them. "You might just find yourself
shakin' under your mama's quilt before we get started
good.

"See there?" Bull said, pointing. "Perty steep bank
to skedaddle over, ain't it? They'll charge this line a time

or two, try to scare us off. Only way they can get us outa this road, though, is to *flank* us, which even them mule-headed Irish'll figure out in time.

"Then things'll get hot, an' I mean *hot*. An' when things *do* get hot–an' they *will* soon enough–you should know for a fact that at two rounds a minute … shit, you might as well be a turkey on a whiskey barrel."

"I ain't runnin' *nowhere!* Look at this line! There're enough rifles pointed t'wards them Yanks to stop the Almighty had *He* a mind to charge." Jacob stood, exposing his head and chest above the breastworks of fence rails.

"*Gitchur ass down, boy!*" shouted another rebel.

Bull looked at Jacob and measured him as a farmer would a mule at auction.

"You cain't be no more'n thirteen, fourteen maybe. What's your unit? How'd you hook up with the Sixth?"

"I'm *sixteen!*" Jacob insisted. "Well … next March, anyhow. Me an' Bigun here come up from Sharpsburg this mornin', over off Landing Road, saw y'all marching through. Y'all looked a might scraggly, an' I said to Bigun, 'these boys need some *help!*' an', well … here we are."

"Sharpsburg?" asked Bull.

"Yep."

"Does Sharpsburg have a right fine restaurant on Main Street, with a maplewood bar polished to the hilt, finest slab of beefsteak east of the Mississip?"

"That's right!"

"An' a general store with a balding man, about forty-five, loves to talk, an' people come from far an'near to play checkers, yak awhile, just to get away from life?"

"Yeah! You *know* Sharpsburg?"

"Never heard of it. Sounds like every small town I've been through since spring of '61."

Jacob sank to the ground and stared through an opening in the fence rails. Bigun grinned.

"Just joshin' with you, boy. I thought you Marylanders didn't want anything to do with us rebs," Bull said, locking his blue eyes onto Jacob's. "We splashed across the Potomac expectin' a rousin' welcome. Instead, we got nothin' but waggin' fingers and shakin' heads."

Jacob said nothing.

"Shit. Boy, you hear me good. In ten minutes, you gawn wish you kept your scrawny little ass home milkin' cows an' shuckin' corn!" Bull shifted his weight from a prone to a kneeling position, ignoring his own advice to keep low. "We need every man, true, but this *ain't* no boy's fight. Not yet, anyway. Let me tell you a thing or two 'bout this war, an' you best take a good listen whilst you got the chance."

Bigun perked up. Jacob stared at the field. Dragonflies hovered over ground.

"You see that ridge out yonder?" Bull asked Jacob, pointing toward the rolling pinnacle of unsuspecting meadow grass cascading on the breeze.

"I see it."

"Soon enough, an army bigger than any you'll ever see's gawn march right over that rise, anxious as us for the fray. They want to see the elephant, just like you. But, just like you, a lot of 'em don't know what the hell that means. Their colors'll be flappin' faster than a thirsty dog's tongue, an' their heads'll be low to the ground, as if that makes 'em less a target, an' perty soon they'll come to the double-quick, each one of 'em knowin' full well, *full damn well*, their last breath is but a short step away.

"They won't stop, though. They'll come on because they understand that dyin's the lesser of the two evils of war."

Bull paused and blew the rye stem to the ground. He stared straight over the waving grass, waiting for his thoughts to catch up with his words.

"Damn mosquitoes!" Jacob said, slapping his arm.

Moment of Truth

"Hell, boy, consider yourself lucky. Mosquitoes ignore me," Bull said, sniffing his body. "I don't know whether I'm blessed or insulted. They smell me an' run."

The two shared a chuckle and a moment of silence.

"Dyin's easier than runnin', boy," Bull continued. "That's a lesson you'll learn if you survive this little scrape. Once that lesson's learned, there ain't no turnin' back. Sounds strange, but a man's gotta have the courage of Job to run," uttered Bull, his voice scratched by the maniacal din of battles prior. Bull squeezed the barrel of his rifle, extracting a measure of comfort, like a child coddling a play-pretty. "Ain't no man got that kind of courage."

Bull wiped the sweat of his palms on the sides of his trousers and adjusted the hat on his head to better deflect the blast of the morning sun. He checked his musket for a percussion cap.

"When they get close enough, right around twenty paces, we're gawn send that first rank to hell. But there's another wave right behind 'em, and another wave still. An' then some. Before long, they'll be too many of 'em. We can hold 'em off for a spell, maybe long enough for Hill to come up from Harper's Ferry, but you can bet your Sweet Jesus ol' McClellan's sendin' a whole division, maybe two, right at this Godforsaken road, an' then … well, then, it's just a matter of time. *That* you can count on! You best be ready for the long sleep, boy, or run like an ol' hare through that cornfield yonder whilst you got the notion."

Captain John Gorman and Colonel Charles Tew, alerted by rebel spotters forward in the fields, trotted the few dozen yards to the crest of the ridge in front of the fence line bordering Hog Trough Road. The enemy was advancing at intervals through farmer Roulette's field, three lines deep and a half-mile wide. The silence of the Confederate officers told the waiting rebels all that needed saying.

136

The blue waves rolled forward, straight and precise, echoes of orders bouncing across the air. Flags snapped. Soldiers in blue marched, lips tight, preparing their bodies as best they could for the impact.

"Whachu mean by–by seein' the elephant?" asked Jacob, reluctant to know the details of an answer he already suspected.

"Ain'chu ever wanted to see a circus elephant?"

"Well … yeah, but–"

"It's a manner of speakin', boy. Goin' into battle's like facing an elephant; it's an awesome sight to behold, the adventure of a lifetime! Except you gawn soon learn enough it ain't the fun of a circus."

Jacob stared at Bull, the tilt of his torn hat a measure of his experience and wisdom. *Adventure of a lifetime*, he thought.

"Seems like you've done perty good so far," Jacob observed. "Why you still doin' it, seein' the elephant, that is? Why risk gettin' killed?"

Bull pried off, then pressed back on, the percussion cap on the nipple of his rifle and turned to Jacob and smiled.

"I got me a wife an' two kids, a boy an' a girl, back home outside Montgomery, Alabama. Used to be I wanted more than anything to see that ol' elephant, to revel in the glory. I loved seein' the wave of a lady's handkerchief an' hearin' the cheers of homefolks wherever we marched. Whippin' them Yanks at Manassas, twice to boot, felt good–felt *real* good–but it set my mind straight."

Bull's eyes narrowed as he clutched a cartridge between his fingers.

"I seen these damned Minies do things to a man I never thought possible to do. I heard the zing and buzz of bullets flyin' through the air like bees at a flower show. I felt the vibrations of their spin on my temple. I heard the crunch, like snowballs on a barn door, bullets striking flesh an' bone of men no more than a hand's length away, an' I wondered *how on God's sweet earth* I was spared. I was surely no saint an' not one ounce more deservin' to live than they was.

"I seen legs an' arms ripped away from men who a second before were yellin' with all the vigor of boys showin' off in a school yard.

"I seen blood pour out of men's necks and heads and chests like red waterfalls.

"I seen desperate, doomed men, eyes big as harvest moons, tryin' to salvage their guts–their *guts*–from the ground and tuck 'em back inside, some laughin' with embarrassment, like a woman who spilled her laundry.

"I seen men cryin' like babies, like *babies*, for their mamas cuddle, men filled with terror as death came.

"I seen a shell tear a man in two, torso from legs. I smelled the shit that come out of men as they took their last breath, an' I smelled the rottin' bodies of men bloated by the sun an' half eaten by maggots, an' I smelled the vomit of survivors changed forever by the sights. That's the elephant no recruiters and politicians want to talk about.

"See, boy, I don't care a wit about seein' the elephant no more. I'm fightin' for my family's name an' my honor. I ain't gawn run from no Yankee, 'cause I know he ain't gawn run from *me*. Duty and country is one thing–personal honor is why I'm on this line, rifle pointed thataway. I don't give a shrively rat's ass about slaves or States' rights. A colored's as much a man as me an' has as much a God-given right to–"

THULK.

Jacob reeled.

A bullet finished Bull's thought, smashing into his forehead, splattering blood, bone, and brain onto Jacob's face and shirt. Bull teetered on his knees, his life shot away, gravity unsure which way to take him. Another bullet tore through the middle of his chest. Bull slumped over Jacob's chest, the flame of life snuffed in an instant.

Trapped by the weight of Bull, Jacob stared a moment, his eyes widened with shock at the lifeless form. He thought of the words spoken seconds earlier, now echoes in Jacob's mind.

"Shit!" Bigun shouted.

With a realization as sudden as Bull's death, Jacob frantically shoved the body down the embankment behind him as if he were shaking off a spider.

Two folded pieces of paper, one scrawled with the name 'Caroline', a red-tinged hole burned through them both, slipped from Bull's shirt pocket and flitted in the breeze among the crouched men. It bounced and tumbled along the dirt and grass until it settled somewhere in Piper's corn, safe for the moment from further sacrilege.

Jacob resumed his position, eyes at ground level, finger on his rifle's trigger, lungs panting, as he scanned the distance for the source of the killing shots.

Soldiers pressed percussion caps into place and pulled back the hammers of their muskets, a sound which resonated down the line like sleet off a tin roof. The moment was come.

"Steady, boys! Aim low!" barked the command repeated down the line.

Ole Whooey lowered his beak and nudged his wing feathers, unable to sleep amid the clamor. Now came the elephant, the adventure, the moment.

Chapter 13

Jacob swept his cotton-dry tongue across his lips. He listened as the body of troops drew nearer, a blue curtain opening an act for which he had rehearsed only the glory of his imaginings.

He patted his pocket for his gold coin. Still there. "This adventure's free, Grandpa," he whispered, refusing to acknowledge that it might cost his life.

Jacob pulled two dried flowers of jasmine from his pocket, gave them a sniff and a kiss, and plugged them into his hair.

"Don't rightly know what's gawn happen here, Jasmine, but I need your luck." One flower fell to the dirt.

His only substantive preparation for battle was his detachment from the antiwar tenets of his Daddy's Dunkard faith. War was what men were born to do, Jacob believed. Hadn't David, a man after God's heart, slain Goliath? Any cause worthy of the distinction was worth defending, worth going to war for, Jacob believed. Jacob wondered upon whose cause God now shone His favor.

War was the great proving ground, the lair of the intrepid and cowards. Jacob felt called. Though tender of age and lacking maturity in reason, he believed his life's duty was to forge a trail of his own. Manhood beckoned, and Jacob responded, the minutia of religion be damned.

Jacob was thrust upon this battle, into this line of rebel fighters, facing the men, perhaps the very man, who had killed Roswell. Maybe this was the opportunity to avenge his friend's death. Maybe God had placed him here for that reason. He sensed eagerness, a passion for retribution. He felt Roswell's tug.

His abrupt thirst for blood was quenched just as suddenly by a surge of fear. Maybe the boundaries of the remainder of his life were contained in this single morning! Bull's were.

He wanted to serve, if only he knew whom to serve and why. He also wanted to flee, if only he knew where. He wanted time to prepare his mind and spirit for such a commitment. What he did not want was to die.

Thoughts swirled in his brain, each one cutting off the other, running together, like a stampede of thunder-scattered cattle. One thing he knew. Claggett and those other two dead men no longer mattered. Vengeance mattered. Rachael mattered. Commitment mattered.

If the South wanted its independence, just as the colonists had sought from the English four score and six years prior, who were the politicos of Washington to stop them? Purity of purpose, Jacob believed, also eluded a government bent on pushing the Indians into the Pacific and wrestling territory from the Mexicans.

Now this same government, headed by an unpopular President, denied Southerners their own brand of manifest destiny, all in the noble name of preserving the Union. Jacob believed the Union had long devolved, putrid like an open jar of sun-baked blueberry jam, an acrid, retching mass, no longer preservable. *Who can be right when everything seems so damn wrong*, Jacob's thoughts shouted.

Jacob's best friend had been shot dead, murdered, by Union soldiers as he waded across the Potomac. They presumed Roswell a Confederate soldier, perhaps a spy. Roswell never got the chance to explain.

Whom to fight against, whom to fight for–the matter for Jacob had taken a turn for the personal. Jacob would be his friend's surrogate, for now.

But Jacob knew that freedom mattered also, for everyone, in a sense larger than had been promoted by the Northern newspapers. Jacob wrestled with his convictions, Union and Secessionist. Slavery, he knew, was a canker upon this country. Bigun mattered.

Despite calls to manhood, Jacob was not eager to bear arms and participate in the national calamity, not for either side, especially after the violent end to his conversation with Bull moments earlier.

Perhaps their finding the Rebel battle line in their line of flight was God's conduit for delivering Jacob. Deliverance *from* guilt; deliverance *to* manhood; deliverance *of* truth.

Jacob caressed his battlefield-found treasure and felt a sort of induction-by-materiel, a debt to military duty. He felt as well the tug to run, to flee through Piper's corn and leave the business of war to those who knew its conduct. If he turned tail now, some Yankee wouldn't give a country damn whether Jacob was a Dunkard, a rebel, an abolitionist, or just a wayward Sharpsburg scarecrow.

All his swirling thoughts boiled down to self-preservation, for everyman the essence of battle. God had chosen sides for him.

He leveled his eye, eyelid aquiver, down the steel-blue barrel of his newfound rifle and fixed his focus upon the middle of some poor bastard's chest pounding with the cadence of a thousand heartbeats, a thousand longings to be elsewhere, *anywhere*, carried by legs edging closer to the precipice.

Jacob had never engaged in a schoolyard scuffle or so much as killed a crow. Before him now marched, and beside him now waited, whole armies of living, feeling, thinking beings, souls far from the securities of home, souls in a spot well past the point of no return.

He thought of the conical gray ounce of lead cradled inanimate in the breech of his rifle, forged from raw material taken from the dust of the earth, destined from the dawn of time to snuff the life of a man with whom he had no tiff, no grudge.

Maybe the man to Jacob's right or left had placed aim against the same poor bastard. His guilt eased a bit. Ole Whooey stared at the distant incoming blue mass, strange invaders of Jacob's and Rachael's courting grounds.

General William French's division, Second Corps, Army of the Potomac, marched southwestward across the undulating open ground between the Mumma and Roulette farms. Light of the mid-morning sun flickered off the array of clanking metallic objects attached to the belts and backs of the approaching troops, like wildfire pushed by the wind. The fields were full of bluecoats marching with the steadiness of the drill, precision preceding tumult.

The rebels were ordered prone; still, some stood and watched in amazement at the parade-like view advancing before them. Some Confederates took long draws from their canteens, perhaps toasts to their brethren across the way, and wiped their mouths and brows with rolled sleeves, for many their final measure of physical comfort.

Some continued to wave their forage caps and slouch hats, and shout cheers of respect to the enemy, men just the same. Others derided the blue lines with verbal stones of discouragement.

Some men flung their flasks of whiskey to the ground, by doing so perhaps gaining some measure of divine favor and adding a chance or two to the credit side of survival.

Opportunists raked up the scattered treasures and stuffed them into trouser pockets, anticipating an outcome worthy of celebration.

More men than not prayed and kissed photographs of homefolk.

"Get us reinforcements; for God's sake, *do it now!*" shouted a Confederate colonel to an aide. The aide bolted rearward. "God be with us," the officer said, gazing through field glasses at the approaching blue tide.

A second line of infantry formed along the southern side of Hog Trough Road and against Piper's cornfield. This line hadn't the protection offered by the sunken road, but the soldiers did have a route of retreat unhampered by the road's slopes.

"Hold your fire until you see the eagles on their breastplates!" shouted another colonel, standing as an example of defiance atop the rear slope of the sector of Hog Trough Road occupied by regiments from North Carolina.

Jacob looked at Bigun, who lay resolute of purpose, rifle sight fixed upon those who would free him. He believed Southern soldiers would spare him as long as he fought beside them, or gave the appearance of such. He knew as well that his color offered no protection from a Yankee bullet.

Jacob turned his head to the serenity of the field behind. Piper's corn beckoned his flight. He thought of the notion Bull spoke about. Hell was about to erupt. If he were going to run, now was the time.

The battle was ended for Bull, blood covering his face and torso like a crimson quilt. No more traipsing around the house and yard with his daughter on his shoulders. No more snug winter nights cuddled close with his beloved under quilts of goose down. No more Sunday picnics in the shaded coves of Boulder River. No more dreams. No more disappointments. No more winters of ravaging illness. No more spring plowings and summer droughts. No more autumn harvests. No more cackling of children's laughter. No more Christmas. No more struggles. No more contentment. No more strife. No more life. Now only peace. If life made little sense for Bull, death was the antidote.

"We–we stayin', Bigun?" Jacob stuttered, shifting his weight from leg to leg, the answer known.

"Got no choice now," Bigun replied, glancing left and right. "If we run, somebody'll shoot us–shoot me. I ain't got no desire fo' a bullet in my back. If dis be my time, I gawn die a man, facin' forward."

"That's sure a passel of devils out yonder," observed Jacob. "Reckon we can whip 'em?"

Bigun looked at Jacob as if he had traded his senses for his rifle.

"It ain't about whippin' *nobody*," Bigun replied. "If I have to kill a Yankee standin' over me with a bayonet to my throat, dat's one thing. But for me, I gawn do all I can to stay outa dis fight, even if I has to lie still under one of dese dead rebs while y'all kills each other. I'm fightin' for *my* survival an' gettin' back to my family. Sounds like you done gone an' joined the CSA, boy."

Jacob stared across the fields and let Bigun's words take root.

"I want to live, too. I ain't got no dog in this hunt neither, except I do know that this line is all that's between them Yanks an' me an' my Daddy's farm. And Rachael."

"See you when it's over," Bigun said after a thoughtful pause. The pair shook hands.

Steady Confederates, no strangers to tight fixes, honed the aims of their muskets as best they could. Pounding pulses resonated through the hands of untested recruits, their rifles trembling with uncertainty.

Bluecoats in the forward ranks, exposed, eyed one another, wondering who might break first. These were McClellan's green troops, fresh from their sit-down coffees with the silk tongues of recruiters. These soldiers were barely trained to shit in the woods, much less load and fire their long guns in the face of buzzing bullets and a determined enemy. These were the expendable ones, meant only to absorb volleys and buy time for the veterans between enemy loadings, time enough to gain a few yards of ground, closer to the enemy, inch by inch. Few in the front waves possessed the witness of the gore of shredded men, the chaos of the churning maelstrom, the fury of flying debris, cursing men, and screaming souls.

Kill them first, the rebels knew, and the greens in the back ranks would scatter like hens. Heads of nervous Yankees turned right and left, gauging their own sense of commitment against that of their equally inexperienced officers. Hearts of frightened men filled to bursting with tension from a knowledge that the coming flash of two thousand muskets would be the last sight they would see on this earth.

The Union waves marched onward. Anxiety had a way of pushing some legs faster than others. The lines bulged in places, producing slight S-curves. Forward they pressed, crushing the grass like a blue wheel.

"Steady, boys!" Colonel John Gordon of the Sixth Alabama barked, his tone as firm and strong as his countenance. "Alabamans never waver!"

"He looks like one mean son of a master," Jacob observed. "An army of one! No wonder ain't nobody runnin'."

"He just another casualty waitin' to happen," Bigun said with a spit. "Look at 'im walkin' dat line like Jesus. Dey's a hunnert Yankee rifles pointed at 'im now if dey's one."

Gordon had come to embody an air of invincibility, not only for his command, but also for the Army of Northern Virginia. He had taken seven bullets through his clothing at the Battle of Seven Pines, none of which pricked his flesh. His men were willing to face any odds as long as Colonel John Gordon held command.

Jacob and Bigun braced for the attack. Features on the faces of Yankees were as clear as the blue sky. Men up and down the lane glanced impatiently at their commanding officers and squirmed to receive the order to fire. Rodes' Alabamans, Anderson's North Carolinians, Colquitt's Georgians, others of patchwork units, all readied for the firestorm. Fingers caressed triggers, a disquiet rising in men desperate to blow backwards the rolling tide.

Yankee banners of green and gold and red and blue, each emblazoned with the stitched names of prior engagements, appeared to rise out of the grass on the crest of the ridge, like Satan's legions.

The soldiers in the road, set for the shoot, gazed with awe at the uniformity and precision of the advance and with respect for the courage upon which they would soon lay waste. A spontaneous cheer arose from the Rebel line. Men stood and waved hats, a gesture of honor from men upon men.

Standard-bearers of the approaching Second Corp waved their proud regimental colors. Onward came the 130th and 132nd Pennsylvania, the 8th Ohio, the 5th Maryland, the 14th Indiana, the 1st Delaware, the 4th New York, and others in the vanguard.

These young boys, many at the pinnacle of their first grand adventure, dipped into a swale of temporary safety, out of sight; a few minutes later they topped the crest of a rise and saw clearly before them countless holes of shining barrels resting on fence rails, rifles pointed motionless at them. Each barrel held a messenger of the Reaper. A sudden, collective shudder gripped the blue ranks, now a fatal thirty yards away, each man aware his moment of truth had arrived.

"Fire!" Colonel Gordon shouted, the veins of his neck bulging with blood.

Moment of Truth

The din of discharging rifles shattered the valley air like the collapse of a hundred glass cities. Muskets spat an unbroken line of flame and smoke. Bullets carved paths through the thick air, spitting dirt and grass, pinging canteens and rifles, and smashing into chests and foreheads and arms and necks and stomachs and knees and thighs and shoulders and faces. Walls of lead lifted men and slammed them in twisted clumps to the ground. Blood surged from hundreds of wounds, coloring the grass and soil with a red sludge.

Jacob held his breath as he loaded his rifle, careful to keep his body low. He looked around. Yankee bullets thunked the wood rails and kicked puffs of dirt in front of Hog Trough Road. Rebels tore paper off cartridges and spat, poured the powder into muzzles, and shoved the lead home. The road filled with sounds of scraping, clinking ramrods, like sandpaper and nails. The blue tide receded.

Chapter 14

"Name's *Tucker!* Tucker McGavin! Second North Carolina!" the teenager shouted, his voice barely audible above the roar. He rammed a ball down the barrel of his .69 caliber smoothbore. "We in a *fight* now, you 'spect?" He held out his bloodstained left hand. "Damn ball took away half my bird finger, jus' as I was given 'em what fer! Ain't much on dressin' wounds under fire! Them sons of bitches is hittin' us left, right, and front. They'll be in our rear 'fore long. What's your name, soldier?"

Jacob hesitated to return his name, realizing that on this day last names meant nothing, and first names were distractions. Conversation was suicidal.

Who the hell can think about talkin' now? thought Jacob, as he plunged powder and ball into his Springfield. *This ain't no goddamn church social!*

Tucker lay on the ground, rifle propped against the breastwork of fence rails, tending his nagging wound. Bullets thunked into fence rails, sending splinters of wood in every direction. He ignored them.

"Jacob!" Jacob relented as he planted a percussion cap onto his rifle's nipple, yanked back the hammer, and fired low and level between the stacked fence rails into the smoke-shielded enemy. He winced as the rifle's butt recoiled into his bruised shoulder.

Moment of Truth

"Man, I'd love to get my hands one of them Sons of Erin flags," Tucker said, referring to the 69th New York of the Irish Brigade. "Just about pulled out of line an' run after it when I seen it fall. If them boys hadn't been so damn close …"

Like a slashing monster with invisible teeth, bullets shattered fence, spit dust, splattered flesh, and crunched bone, sending pieces of debris spinning through the air like seeds in a spring storm. This vortex of violence filled with screams, orders, pleas, curses, leaden smoke, lead and iron. How anyone remained unscathed was no less than a miracle. As long as hands could hold them, regimental colors waved side to side, daring the enemy to advance. The enemy obliged. Unseen bullets slapped buntings and thumped bodies.

"They comin' at us from over yonder," shouted Tucker, pointing front-left towards a knoll adjacent to Roulette's lane, "an' directly yonder; an' they's artill'ry somewheres over that rise there, lobbin' shells, knockin' the *shit* outa us!

A soldier next to Tucker turned right, his attention grabbed by events at the end of the line of battle toward the Fourth and Thirtieth North Carolina regiments. As he pointed, a ball slammed into his throat, ripping away half his neck. Blood gurgled then gushed like a torrent through a downspout. A flash of terror, truth, crossed the man's face, and then he was gone.

"*Goddamn* flankin' fire!" erupted Tucker, wiping away splotches of the man's blood. "Here they come!"

Tucker licked his thumb, cocked the hammer, stood and delivered a shot into the ranks of the 64th New York, part of Barlow's command bearing down on the right flank of the beleaguered Confederate line. He stood firm, erect in defiance of the enemy, and repeated the arduous process of loading. Men reeled and jerked and dropped in the sea of carnage. Tucker did not flinch.

Jacob yelled, "What them fellas yonder cheerin' about?" referring to a mass of waving caps on the ridge to the road's front.

"God knows what! Hell, they prob'ly jus' glad they's *able*," Tucker grunted, firing his rifle.

Bullets zinged and zipped past Jacob's ears, and he marveled at his good fortune for having avoided blocking their path. Jacob felt surrounded by a vacuum of immortality, an audacious sensation that even point-blank shots were as peas against his shield of Thor.

Perhaps today was not Jacob's day to die. Perhaps his survival was sheer birthright, a prosperity granted by the gods of war. He looked behind him and saw Colonel Gordon, bleeding from his right leg and left shoulder, hobbling back and forth, spurring his men to hold the line, ignoring his perilous injuries as best he could, standing not only as an example of courage for his men but as a distraction for Yankee rifles.

"Jesus, look at that man!" shouted Jacob, pointing to Gordon.

"He's taken two or three bullets meant fer you, Jacob," Tucker replied. "Be grateful an' load up!"

Colonel Gordon hobbled. He stopped and glanced at the noon sun and wiped his brow.

Jacob saw the sunken road filling with bodies and parts of bodies. He smelled the stench, the gut-wrenching contents of dead and dying men. He heard the laughter of maniacs, the screams of men burning with unthinkable pain, each comforted once upon a time by the song and sunshine of the Potomac crossing and the thought that when battle came, death would find the other man.

Now men flailed to fend off the inevitable, as one might spin and dance and curse in the repulse of hornet swarms. Jacob heard the agony of voices pleading for mamas and girlfriends, for security well out of reach yet well within the forefronts of fading minds.

Moment of Truth

He watched the cheering enemy. They kept coming. Coming still, a blue flood, all but drowning the rebel defenses. In this fight of attrition, the numbers favored the Federals. Men pillaged cartridge boxes for ammunition and the ground for stones, savage quests to cannibalize anything worth flinging at the coming hordes. The rebel gods of battle raked their hands across scabbards and their fingers inside quivers, desperate for miracles. Even the supernatural had no answer.

"Shoot your Goddamned gun!" Tucker roared.

Musket fire pattered all around as men hugged the soil and pulled dead comrades close to rest their rifles upon and to absorb incoming rounds. The air was furious, a stained, sulfuric sarcophagus.

Jacob, oblivious to his pause, rested his head against a pockmarked fence rails. Smoke shrouded him like a specter. He stared blankly at the madness, dazed, given to his newfound invulnerability. Bullets pinged rifle barrels, clipped wooden posts, and ripped through loose clothing. Men were lifted off the ground by simultaneous impacts, their bodies shredded to ghastly pulp. Tucker grabbed Jacob's weapon and pulled the hammer.

"Gimme a damn cap!" Tucker shouted.

His motion mechanical, Jacob handed Tucker a percussion cap. Tucker pressed the cap onto the nipple and shoved the rifle back to Jacob.

"Best you git back in this fight, boy! Might as well take some of them yankity-yanks with us, 'cause sure as the sun is high, this road's our grave!"

Tucker loaded and fired with superhuman speed. The firing lines of Gaines Mill, Mechanicsville, and Manassas had taught him to keep the enemy as pinned as possible. Seldom came opportunities for selective aiming. Anything that moved was a target. The direction of the enemy, often a guess, was the target.

Hog Trough Road presented a damning twist. The enemy had thrown two divisions at the sunken farm lane, the center of Lee's line. The road bent in its center, exposing the rebel line to enfilading crossfire on either side of the angle.

Now the Yankees were firing down the right flank of the road as well. Caldwell's brigade, shooting down-slope of the road, blistered the reeling line of rebels. Bullets smacked Confederates from three directions. Bodies falling in one direction were at once jerked in another. The situation worsened to the point of panic. Still, the rebels held.

Colonel Gordon's head snapped back. A fifth ball struck under his left eye, exiting out the right side of his neck. He slammed to the ground, face down inside his hat.

Jacob glanced to either side in search of Bigun. He noticed an object moving in his periphery, lifted his rifle, and fired at the blue blur of a soldier hurdling the fence breastwork. Jacob felt a sting punch his left chest, staggering him. He brushed his hand over the area. Finding no blood, consciousness intact, he reached for a cartridge.

As he loaded his rifle, Jacob noticed the brown skin of a man's leg protruding from under a stack of bodies. "Bigun!" he shouted. *"Bigun!"*

Jacob knew. His first instinct was to pull away the bodies. He thought better, realizing a dead man was beyond help.

As had been the case all morning for the rebels, officers ordered men from the strongest positions to relieve the severest points of stress along the firing line. Such was now the case as Yankees of Barlow's 64th/61st New York and Caldwell's 5th New Hampshire applied untenable pressure on the Confederate right in the sunken road. The Yankees were in the road; the rebels were being flanked.

Moment of Truth

Orders were shouted to men from the 6th Alabama
to meet the new Union threat. In the din of noise, this order
was mistaken for a call to abandon the road for the safety of
Piper's corn and the Hagerstown Pike beyond. Other
regiments noticed men streaming rearward and, in their
panic, followed suit. The demise of rebel defenses in the
Hog Trough Road was complete.

"Everybody's skedaddlin', Tucker! Look!" Jacob
shouted.

"Look out, you damn fool!" Tucker shouted as he
tilted his musket at an angle, the barrel under the chin of a
charging Yankee. The Yankee pointed a revolver at
Jacob's head, but before he could pull the trigger, Tucker
pulled his, decapitating the officer.

Jacob looked at Tucker and managed a slight,
shaken smile of gratitude just as another officer's sword
impaled Tucker from mid-back through the belly. Tucker's
eyes widened with shock as he fell to his knees, hands
gripping the curved blade. Blood rushed from the wound
and trickled out his mouth.

The officer pushed Tucker to the ground with his
boot, yanking the sword from Tucker's body. He raised his
sword to repeat the process on Jacob but was met with a
Bowie thrust into his chest. Tucker released the Bowie's
handle. He gave Jacob a smile as he fell face down.

Rebels raced through Piper's cornfield, a mad run to
escape certain death in the road. Some men ran backwards,
afraid of attracting a bullet in the back. Others kneeled and
managed to fire a round or two before falling back. Lee's
center had collapsed.

Yankees poured into the road, stepping on bridges
of rebel corpses and wounded. Jacob froze. He wanted to
run but could not muster the nerve to chance it. He knelt in
the ice of indecision. He watched soldiers strain to
scramble up the steep southern embankment of Hog
Trough, desperate to escape the onslaught. Most did not

make it. As he reached for his Springfield, a bullet zipped though his body just below his left shoulder. Jacob fell amid heaps of dead Confederates, next to Tucker.

Chapter 15

Men and materiel flailed in a macabre dance of motion. Writhing wounded gasped for air, moaned for water, begged for a merciful end. Men locked in the throes of death sought one last frantic measure of comfort, anything to curb the hell of their reality. Others rested on the ground and atop comrades, chests heaving with an acceptance of the unthinkable: gut-shot; chest-shot; limbs shattered or shot away; futures riding the swift flow of blood to the soil.

Jacob raked his hands across his torso in a feverish search for his wound. He felt only the warm squish of his blood-dampened shirt. Beside him lay a standard-bearer of the Sixth Alabama, the unclaimed trophy draped like a sheet over his bullet-splattered body.

Hog Trough Road churned like a hacked snake. The bulk of the fighting shifted to discordant attacks in Mumma's fields a hundred yards north-northeast of the road and to Piper's corn a few hundred yards south of the road. Soldiers of the Seventh Maine screamed with the voice of victory as they leaped over the bodies in the road. Their objective was a mob of fleeing Confederates regrouping in the orchards of Piper's farm, survivors of Anderson's and Rode's brigades thrown together in desperate haste to stem the hurl from Hog Trough Road and to save Lee's army, the Confederacy itself.

Jacob pulled the banner free of its shaft and pressed the wadded cloth inside his shirt against the ooze. The flag's field of red and Jacob's blood mingled. He laid back his head and awaited death to still dreams born of innocence.

Little attention was given the injured Rebels in the road aside from the occasional sympathetic Union soldier who lowered his canteen to the enemy's lips. No one noticed the prize of Jacob's wound dressing, indistinguishable from his bloodstained shirt. No one except Bigun.

Bigun emerged from beneath the cover of dead soldiers. He was unscathed and intended to remain so. The last of the pursuing Yankees scampered across the road. Bigun raised to his knees and scanned the horror surrounding him. Bullets meant for other targets zipped through the air and thunked the dead and wounded mounded in the road.

Bigun knew that most of these men, mostly boys, owned no slaves and were not fighting this war to preserve the right. These men had learned their bravery as they had learned their bigotry. These were men caught in the vortex of ideologies and the spin of conflicting ideas. Geopolitical boundaries meant little to these men. Only survival mattered. These men of blue and gray represented the essence of a young America, an essence that valued courage and bravado, even death, over cowardice or surrender. These men understood that singular sacrifice ensured collective survival. Bigun wondered if he were so brave to fight his battle for freedom.

He glanced around in search of Jacob. The pools of blood and mangle of flesh made recognition of human features and individuals next to impossible. Eyes stared heavenward. Mouths gaped, frozen in their realization.

Bigun counted sixteen bullet holes in the body of a color-bearer. Those were the wounds he could see. He noticed the shaft stripped of its flag, undoubtedly now a Yankee trophy.

The cacophony of misery rang in Bigun's ears like the peal of hell's bells. He saw a lumpy blotch of red tucked sloppily under a boy's shirt. The boy turned his face toward Bigun.

"Jacob!" Bigun said with a gasp.

Bigun scrambled over a few corpses and reached Jacob. He touched the sticky flag and gently peeled it back. He saw Jacob's eyes blink, his chest rise and fall slightly, evidence his friend was alive. Bigun lifted the flag and viewed the wound. He wiped away thick blood and dabbed the flow of fresh blood. The wound was silver-dollar sized. Bigun ignored the dash of Yankees scrambling past, each distracted by the chore of maneuvering the body-strewn road.

"Lawd have mercy," Bigun said repeatedly.

"How bad, Bigun?" Jacob mumbled.

"Bad," Bigun replied, reaching his fingers under Jacob's back inspecting for an exit wound. You lost a lot of blood, but least it ain't comin' outcha mouth, so I reckon your lungs ain't hit. Bullet went clean th'ough."

Jacob smiled. "One heck of an elephant. You–you get hit?"

"Naw. I found me a body to ...." Bigun checked his answer and changed the subject. "Jacob, I gots to gitchu out from here. I gots to gitchu home!"

"How you gawn do that, Bigun? Fightin' ain't stopped."

The sounds of battle had diminished little. Home was about a mile west of the apex of Hog Trough Road, a beeline beyond the Hagerstown Pike across the stubble and grass of the Reel farm and then the Landing Road.

Bigun hesitated amid the melee but supposed no one would shoot a man helping the wounded off the field. He perused the immediate ground for a swatch of white cloth. Finding nothing of so innocent a color, he ripped a piece from his sweat-stained shirt, tied the cloth around a broken ramrod, and plunged the ramrod through the frizz of his hair. The cloth shimmied in the breeze.

He reached down and lifted Jacob, praying aloud the Lord to deflect the stream of stray bullets whizzing like flies, and began a trot westward across no-man's-land toward the Hagerstown Pike.

Bigun bent over, shielding Jacob and keeping a low profile, as he stepped across the field toward the Pike. Rebel artillery sprayed canister and stemmed the enemy's advance.

The patchwork line of Rebels along the Pike stood and raised their caps and hats, cheering the approaching pair to the relative safety of a waist-high stone wall. Bigun stepped over the wall and passed through the line of soldiers, all blackened with powder and sweat, some administering wounds with tourniquets or cornhusks. He felt scarcely safer behind the new Rebel line, given the carnage in Hog Trough Road and the likelihood the Yankees would resume the assault.

"What–whatchu gawn tell my Daddy?" Jacob asked Bigun.

"Reckon I won't have to do much tellin'," Bigun said between quick breaths. "Mr. Isaac got ears like all us folk. He knows dey's a battle in dese fields, but I spect once he sees dis reb flag dressin' up yo' wound, he's gawn ask a few questions. Course, then, he might jus' go ahead an' put another bullet in you once he hears whatchu gots to say.

"Whatchu gawn tell 'im, anyhow?" Bigun asked, returning the question. "He gawn know you been *in* the fight, not jus' a innocent boy who happened to stop a bullet. B'sides, you gots enough powder on yo' face to pass as my kin. I reckon you all sent a few of dem Yankee boys to their glory."

Jacob and Bigun laughed as they swished through the grass.

"Yeah, we did, but ain't a one of us can put no flag staff in *our* hair," Jacob retorted.

Both men laughed harder. Jacob winced with the pain of the laugh-aggravated wound.

"Where's my rifle?" Jacob asked.

"Where's yo' rifle?" Bigun asked, incredulous, his lip curled and eyes squinted. "Boy, you lucky to have yo' *life*. Come back tomorrow, hell, next week, an' pick up all de rifles you want! Ax me sump'n else."

"What we gawn do with this reb flag, Bigun?"

"You want me to th'ow it away?"

"Hell, no!" Jacob said. He coughed. "I took a bullet for the South, for Roswell, an' I aim to keep my payment."

"But, Mr. Isaac, he'll-"

"I don't give a rat's cheese about what my Daddy thinks of this war, or me, anymore. I've made my decisions. But I do reckon he'll burn this flag if he gets hold of it. Bigun, you got to hide it for me. You got to take …"

"*Me?* Me hide a *rebel* flag? Lemme check yo' head for wounds. Whatchu think my people'll do to me if dey finds dis here flag in my possession? Shit, I might as well pluck de feathers an' stir de tar pot myse'f."

Jacob chuckled. "You're right, you're right. Still, I don't want to lose this trophy. What's it say on it?"

"You *has* lost a lot of blood! How on God's sweet earth you spect me to read when ain't nobody *teached* me?"

"How's the bleedin'?" Jacob asked.

Bigun rested Jacob against a tree stump and gently removed the flag from the wound.

"Stopped, fo' now," he replied.

"Good. Hurts like a sonofa–"

"Hold on!" Bigun said. "Ain'chu got no respec' fo' yo' mama, mamas everywhere?"

"Seems to me I earned the right."

"Not around me, you ain't!"

"Okay, okay. Hurts like *the devil*. Can you take the flag off and spread it on the ground?"

Bigun heard the blasts of artillery and the shatter of musketry east of the Pike. He believed it only a matter of a short while before their spot was overrun by retreating Confederates, none of whom would show a smidgeon of sympathy for Jacob's possession of so solemn a symbol. Looking over his shoulder, Bigun spread the flag on the ground. Jacob sat stunned at the volume of blood, mostly his, covering the flag. He felt dizzy. He read the few visible letters painted along the edges of the banner, evidence of the regiment's prior engagements.

"S–E–V sump'n, sump'n, P, sump'n, I–N … S;
G–A–I … S … M … L–L;
M–A–N–A … S."

Dozens of gray-rimmed holes pierced this flag, jagged points of red and blue cloth hanging, clinging, confirmation that an army's colors was the soul of its will. Kill the standard-bearer, pierce the soul. Pierce the soul, wither the will. Unarmed men, hoisting in the savage midst the symbol of all the reasons worth fighting for, had fallen, their only defense a shield of flesh and their will.

Jacob had spent the past three hours in a quagmire of violence. But his blood painted this flag with searing commitment, just like Roswell. He had seen the elephant, ridden it standing up, just as Roswell had yearned to do. And lived.

Chapter 16

Bigun's trot across the Reel fields ebbed to a quickened walk. Jacob's weight felt heavier with each step. Bigun ignored his cramping muscles and dared not set down his cargo again. The thunder of artillery rolled across the fields and through the trees. The gray haze of battle covered the valley, hiding the sun and choking memories of peace. The whole countryside festered in a hellish brew of bodies and debris.

Jacob said nothing. Blood loss had sapped his energy. Bigun noticed the son of his master was unconscious, a good thing, he thought, given the severity of his wound. The bleeding had subsided, despite the shaking of the trot over uneven terrain.

As Bigun approached the Reel farm, shells fell and exploded all around the barn and surrounding buildings. Federal artillery, perhaps their long-range pieces across the Antietam, had a bead on the structures. Forward-bent stretcher-bearers entered and exited the barn, ferrying their wounded loads to hopelessly overburdened surgeons and returning to the canvas of carnage.

Orders barked on the grounds surrounding the barn as companies of soldiers formed ranks. Shells screaming and exploding, the men hastened from this staging area to the fields abandoned by Bigun moments earlier.

Bigun stopped to catch his breath. He had considered taking Jacob to Reel's barn but thought better of it. No patch of earth seemed out of harm's reach. He filled his lungs with air and started his trot toward home. The crunch of timbers and an explosion rocked his cadence as he reached the fence along the Landing Road.

Turning toward the sound, he saw the barn ravaged by fast-spreading flames, its mobile living in full flight. He heard screams within, punctuation to the injury of so grievous an insult. Some of the helpless were carried out, but the fire raced through the dry, hay-filled barn like wolves through a buffet.

Military traffic filled Landing Road. Reserves of infantry, what few remained, headed east toward the Hagerstown Pike. An endless flow of wounded, stragglers, and deserters slowed the fresh troops. Bigun maneuvered his way through the human tide, still holding firm his friend.

Jacob's house was awash with activity, bloodied men hauled within its walls, dead men carried out. Aides hurried with the removal of doors from their hinges. These they placed atop barrels and sawhorses for service as surgeons' operating tables.

Red water tossed through opened windows sloshed to the ground. Surgeons wiped scalpels on their aprons, accumulating ghastly smears of blood. Calls for linens, water, mamas, and home rose above the din of those who could no more than groan.

Stunned in jaw-dropping disbelief, Bigun approached Jacob's home, *his* home. Scores of wounded carpeted the yard. The gut-shot and chest-shot were set aside, awash in agony and arid of hope, their deaths imminent. Soldiers wounded in their extremities were given priority.

"Put 'im down here, nigger, and get the hell out of my way!" said one of the attendants preparing the wounded.

Bigun stooped and placed Jacob against the trunk of a beech tree. He stirred.

The attendant took a cursory glance at Jacob's wound, ignoring the flag bandage, and scampered to a wagon to help offload a fresh group of injured.

"Wh-where am I? Bigun?"

"I'm right here, Jacob. We's home now. You gawn be fine," he said with a reassuring smile.

"Home?" Jacob said, reaching to rise. "*My* home? "Where's Daddy? Rachael!"

"Be still now, you hear? Ain't nobody here but doctors and wounded. We's lucky we gots *dem*. They's turned yo' house into a hospital. Ain't no place like home to heal a man's hurt."

Jacob smiled, then grimaced. "Hurts like a son of a *bitch*. There. I *said* it!"

Bigun returned a smile.

"Where you reckon my Daddy is?" Jacob asked.

"I spect he skedaddled once the fightin' started," Bigun answered, wondering the same about his family. "Couldn't stay in dat chu'ch like he said him an' Mistuh Samuel was gawn do."

"No, not Daddy," Jacob asserted. "He vowed never to let this place fall into Rebel hands, lest he died first." Jacob paused. "Reckon they killed him?"

"Shaw, no!" Bigun replied. "Even yo' daddy cain't hold off the whole Rebel army, an' he ain't fool enough to try. I reckon he went down to Otto's or maybe even to Boonsboro, to wait dis thing out. He'll be along after while."

"You think them three men are amongst all the dead soldiers?"

Bigun gazed at the horror swirling about him. An arm sailed out a window, followed by a leg, and fell amid piles of other severed limbs. The stench of blood and flesh–death–gradually overtook the pervasive odor of sulfur and spent powder.

Men screamed their desperate defiance in the ears of doctors resigned to the inevitable treatment for a shattered bone. The effects of chloroform soon subdued them, and the dreadful work began. Aides winced as surgeons, grim-faced and overwhelmed with blood, bent over their patients and yanked bow saws to and aft with feverish rapidity. Others gripped amputation knives between their teeth as they lifted torn bodies onto door tables.

"Bigun?" Jacob said.

"What? Oh, dem men. You talkin' 'bout Claggett and dem other two? I reckon ain't nobody gawn know 'em from any other dead man out there. Don't worry yo'self about dat no mo'."

"How bad does it look?" Jacob asked again. "My wound."

Bigun lifted the blood-red banner, careful not to disturb coagulated bleeders.

"It ain't lookin' all dat bad," Bigun lied. "Fact is, you is alive and talkin'. Dem doctors'll clean you up, slap on a bandage, and you'll be shootin' pum'kins off fence posts befo' you know it. You in a lot better way dan most of dese men."

Jacob smiled. "Liar!"

"Whatchu want me to do wit' dis flag, boss?"

"Tuck it under your shirt and–and take it–take it across the road to that big sycamore down the road a piece, the one with the lightnin' strike. You know the one I'm talkin' about? The one with the hollow at the base?"

Bigun thought a moment. "I knows it."

"Put it there, down deep in that hollow. Don't you say *nothin'* to *nobody* about it, you hear me?"

Bigun bent over Jacob to conceal his actions. He took the flag, fashioned a quick fold and stuffed it under his shirt.

"Step aside, nigger!" shouted an aide. Bigun froze. "Lemme look atchu, boy," the soldier said, peeling back Jacob's shirt.

Surprised by the sudden command, Bigun stood, careful to keep his hands tightly against his shirt. He slowly stepped his way over and around bodies toward Landing Road. Jacob closed his eyes as the attendant splashed a water-soaked sponge on his chest. He lifted Jacob onto his right side.

"Went clean through you. You one lucky son of a bitch. Most of these boys here caught one in an arm or leg. Docs cain't do much for them fellers except saw the blame things off. Most others are just too damn hurt, an' well … Hey, you cain't be more'n thirteen, fourteen years old."

"Fifteen," Jacob corrected. "Nearly sixteen."

"Hey, you!" the soldier shouted toward two stretcher-bearers. "He'p me git this boy upstairs!" The soldier dabbed the holes with more water. "You're one we can save. Wound's near enough to your shoulder, an' it don't appear to have shattered any bone. I got jus' the place fer ya. Hurt much?"

"Like a *son of a bitch*," Jacob said, feeling a battle-won freedom of expression coursing through his torn body.

The soldiers lifted Jacob and carried him through the congestion and squalor of the parlor, the sounds of dying, suffering men in each room, covering every inch of usable floor space, surgeons and attendants scurrying about like ants. Jacob recognized the shadowed, reddened house as his, but the contents were either removed for the space they occupied or dismantled for their medical use. Some things were plundered outright.

"Get that body off that bed! *Now!*" the aide shouted like a colonel in the field.

The soldiers placed Jacob on the stained bed, Jacob's bed. The private washed the wound of fresh blood, revealing a hole an inch and a half in diameter between the left shoulder and breast.

"Whew! I can just about see right through you. Got to close them holes, boy," the aide said.

Jacob looked at the aide, a mere boy himself.

"That's right. Me."

"But you ain't–"

"All the sawbones are downstairs tendin' to the amputations." The aide pulled a flask of brandy from his pocket and yanked the cork. "Take a swaller or two of this. Ain't got no opium to spare."

Jacob turned the flask up, his first taste of spirits, and drew the contents like water. He lurched and coughed, spraying brandy and saliva. Fresh blood oozed from his wound.

"Damn, boy, go *easy!*" the aide scorned, grabbing the flask and taking a swallow. "What I mean is, well, we ain't got a whole lot of that brandy to go 'round." The aide cleared Jacob's wound of visible bits of clothing and dabbed it with water. "Where you from, soldier?"

"'Round here," Jacob answered, a rote reply to a question he had been asked often this day.

Jacob felt a pinch as the aide inserted a sewing needle into Jacob's shock-numbed skin. He coursed saliva-moistened thread through the eyelet, knotted it and pulled it through Jacob's skin. He repeated the crude process, narrowing the opening with each tug.

"Sharpsburg? Shit, you at *home!* If a soldier's gawn be shot in this goddamned war, ain't no better place to be!"

"*This* is my home, right *here!* You're standin' on its floors," Jacob revealed as the numbness subsided and the pain grew.

"Yeah, sure, an'–hold *still!*–an' Marse Robert's my Daddy!" the aide replied dryly. He placed strips of cloth on the sewn holes and wrapped Jacob's chest and back with linen bandages. "Daddy Robert'll be by directly with some buttermilk biscuits an' gravy, bacon, and hot coffee. I'll be sure to bring you some up." The aide chuckled, pleased with his sarcasm.

"You don't understand. This house is–"

"I understand plenty, soldier. Just you rest up an' maybe some of that *delirium* will go away. I got more wounded than a hive's got bees, an' judgin' from the sound of things," the aide observed, pulling back a curtain and glancing outside, "we might soon be behind Union lines."

"But–"

"No 'buts'! Rest!" the aide insisted as he wrenched the cork off his flask of brandy. "A drink for the living," he boasted, gesturing the flask toward Jacob and gulping the liquid. He paused, wiping his mouth. "And a toast to the dead." He took another swallow and left the room.

Jacob stared at the ceiling. The pain worsened. He imagined the agony of the men downstairs, most with arms and legs shot away, bones splintered beyond repair, wounded in places heretofore inconceivable, and facing the shock of amputation and worse. Shouts and screams drowned out the patter of musket fire and the whine of hot shells. Men no longer fought for any cause except relief, their secessionist glory forgotten.

Jacob realized he was not alone. Unconscious men spotted the floor around him. Some appeared dead. A few hummed unrecognizable tunes, their eyes shut tight and chins uplifted, images of another time their only comfort. Jacob closed his eyes and tried to sleep. He was startled by a voice, a familiar female voice, coming from the hallway outside his room.

"Rachael?"

Delirium.

Chapter 17

"Ma'am? Water." the orderly repeated, his hand on her shoulder.

"Sir? Oh, yes, right away," Rachael said as she lifted the hem of her skirt, enough to clear the bodies. She scuttled to the house.

Rachael returned with an urn of water and a tin cup.

"Ma'am, they gawn need you to make bandages. Any clothes in that house, get 'em an' rip 'em, fast. All sizes. Now."

Without a word, Rachael raced back inside and pulled from a closet clothes belonging to Jacob's deceased mother. Isaac had set them aside after her death and demanded they remain hanging, in case, as he had believed, "Mama should need them." Rachael once thought the gesture romantic. She looked at the wardrobe for a reflective moment, then pulled the clothes down and began the shredding.

Arms cuddled around bundles of stripped cloth, pieces falling to the floor, Rachael scurried up the stairs, her back brushing the wall to allow passage of wounded taken to spaces reserved for post-operative recovery. She heard, but ignored, the sound of her name called from an upstairs room. More pressing concerns demanded her attention as she shuffled down the stairs. Then she stopped

straight up, with the suddenness of an epiphany, body
stilled and eyes wide. She turned.

"Jacob?" she whispered.

She listened for the call to come again, her mind
silencing the cacophony of madness around her. She heard
nothing. Shaking her head, she continued down the stairs
and toward a surgeon standing over a breakfast table.

Wounded men consumed every speck of floor space
in Isaac Hoffman's home. In a corner propped a man
barely conscious, shot through his genitals. Next to him
sprawled a soldier with two bullet holes in his abdomen,
entrails exposed. He mumbled unintelligible words, tears
streaming down his face.

Overcome, Rachael knelt, dropping the strips of
cloth, and strained to discern the man's gibberish. Even
Rachael knew this was a man not long destined for this
world. Her eyes filled with grief for the man. She
wondered what he was telling her, his eyes fixed upon hers
and his limp fingers reaching for her cheek. His expression
was hypnotic. Rachael became desperate to learn the
man's thoughts, his feelings, in his final moments of life.

Another man complained of his inability to clamber
out of the hole in which he stood—until he was told both his
legs had been shot away.

Still another had no jaw, eyes darting side to side
like a child peering over a red wall.

A bullet had carved a groove along the side of a
man's skull, exposing his brain.

The home of the peaceful Dunkard family now
echoed the strains of war, the chords of discord.

"What are you saying? I'm here. Shhh. Tell me,
tell me now. I'm listening," Rachael said to the gut-shot
man.

"Virginia? Virginia, is that—is that you, Virginia?"
the man muttered in an effort swamped with agony. He
pressed his hand against the air.

"No, I'm Rach–yes, yes, it's Virginia. Tell me what you're feeling. What's happening to you, this minute?" Rachael begged, torn between sorrow for the man's fate and her need to understand the death engulfing her.

The man touched Rachael's cheek, softly stroking it.

"I smell cornbread, Virginia. Thank you for your bread ... Virginia," he gasped, his last breath pushing aside Rachael's bangs.

"You there! Bandages!" shouted a surgeon's assistant.

Rachael set the man's stilled hand upon his chest, over his heart. She scooped the strips of cloth and rushed to the table.

Atop the breakfast table sprawled a Union soldier, a sergeant from the 69th New York. The surgeon's aid removed the soldier's forage cap, its green sprig of boxwood falling to the floor and trampled underfoot. An assistant finished shearing the soldier's pants to his waist, the shreds of blue trouser waving with the quiver of activity. His left leg was a red pulp, a jagged hole through his knee. His right hand lay half-clenched on the table, shattered at the wrist. Barely conscious, he muttered, "Faugh-a-Ballagh! Faugh-a-Ballagh!"

"What's he saying?" Rachael asked, sweeping aside the soldier's sweat-drenched black hair and dabbing his forehead.

The surgeon reached into his knapsack, hands smeared with blood, and removed a vial of chloroform. He gave it to his aid. "Clear the way!" the surgeon explained in answer to Rachael's question. "How appropriate."

The aide dripped some chloroform onto a cloth cone and held it to the soldier's nose.

"Faugh-a-Ballagh! Faugh-a-Ballagh!" he shouted again, thrashing, slinging blood and bits of bone onto Rachael's dress. He attempted standing, an out-of-mind reaction to the sleep-inducing chemical. Two assistants restrained him.

"He's still in the fight," said an aid.

"I know how he feels," the surgeon observed, scanning the scores of wounded on the floor and grounds. "Where'd he come from?"

"Don't know. Stretcher-bearers brought him in from across the Hagerstown Pike. Helluva fight over yonder. Said blue and gray littered the ground like autumn leaves."

"Don't our boys know a Yankee when they see one?"

"Some of the men said he was givin' water to our wounded when he was shot. Thought it only fittin' to bring him in. Don't 'spect he'll mind his life saved by a Confederate doctor."

"I reckon not. Got him under?"

The aid lifted the soldier's eyelids. "Like a baby, sir. Flap?"

The surgeon nodded. "Let me have the long knife."

"B. F. Brooks, 69th New York," said Rachael.

"What?" asked the distracted surgeon.

"His name. B. F. Brooks. Pinned to his blouse."

"He's lucky. At least this one's got a name."

The soldier slid his left hand until it touched Rachael's hand. He held two of her fingers as Rachael stared at his closed eyes. She squeezed his hand and looked at the surgeon.

"He's under," the surgeon said. "Reflex, that's all. He would have grabbed a snake had it been there."

The surgeon pinched the skin and muscle of the soldier's thigh and guided the amputation knife through the leg until he struck bone. Tap, tap. Rachael winced at the gruesome sight, turning her head but maintaining her view of the procedure. Blood streamed onto the table and dripped to the floor, broadening the slick coverage of red slime. The surgeon sliced through the muscle in an upward angle, producing a flap of flesh with which to wrap the stump upon removal of the bone. The surgeon repeated the procedure on the underside of the thigh.

"God help him!" Rachael whispered, suppressing as best she could her rising nausea.

Minutes passed. Both flaps were lifted back revealing the bone. An aide handed the surgeon a capital saw. He began the crunching, gnawing process of the amputation, arm racing fore and aft like a lumberjack, the indifference of repetition washing his face. The leg fell free, the ghastly stump more frightful in its removal than the mangled knee moments earlier. Aids cleaned the stump, sutured the flaps, and applied adhesive plaster.

The surgeon wiped wet blood from his hands onto his apron, sighed, and then removed the soldier's right hand with the swift, practiced stroke of perfection.

He listened to the shifting decibels of battle and watched for a moment the endless exodus of wounded carted up the Landing Road toward the Hoffman home.

"My God," he said, the shrieks of devilish agony filling his ears, "what have we done? Next!"

The soldier's leg and hand were tossed out the window, falling atop heaps of other anonymous limbs, their usefulness ruptured, their fullness destroyed.

"Let's get him upstairs, out of the way. Doc needs this table!" shouted an aide.

"May I come?" Rachael asked the soldiers.

"Come on! And bring some water," one answered. "This boy'll be comin' to directly, and he'll be wantin' a perty face to look upon."

Rachael applied a wet compress on the sergeant's forehead. She smiled. Despite the necessary savagery of surgery, he rested with calm. He felt no pain now. Rachael wiped away the smear of black powder and sweat from his straight nose and dimpled chin.

B. F. Brooks, she thought. *You cain't be more than nineteen, twenty.*

"In here! On the floor under the window," said a soldier, directing placement. "Careful. Watch your step."

"Watch over these boys, Rachael. We got us some of Hood's Texans in here. They took a thrashin up near Miller's place this morning. Maybe you can hum "Yellow Rose of Texas" or maybe even "Aura Lea", somethin to lift the spirit."

"A *Yankee* song?" asked a surprised Rachael.

"Got us a Yankee, too, remember?" the soldier said, pointing to the sergeant. "I reckon most of these boys done seen their last sunrise anyhow. They gawn need a "maid of golden hair" to look upon and listen to and remind them of the pleasures of home. Water now."

"Yes, of course," Rachael acknowledged as she turned to retrieve a pitcher of water.

"Rachael," a voice spoke.

Rachael turned. She gawked in surprise upon the sight of Jacob on his own bed, a blood-soaked bandage wrapped around his chest and shoulder.

"Jacob! My God, *Jacob!* It *was* you! What on earth has *happened* to you?"

Jacob managed a smile and a chuckle. "Stepped in the way of a Yankee bullet. Reckon I slowed it down. You should see the other feller!"

I've seen the other fellow, Rachael thought. "But *how?* Where? Have you been in this God-forsaken fight? Jacob, dear Jacob, your chest!"

"Rachael, I just need–I just need some rest. And water."

"Water! Yes. Right here," Rachael said, shocked with her discovery.

Rachael dipped a porcelain cup into the basin of water and placed it against Jacob's lips. She tipped it slightly, allowing a few steady drops into his mouth. Jacob reached with both hands for the cup before withdrawing in pain.

"Ahhh! Son of a–"

"Slowly, Jacob!"

"But I'm just so damned *thirsty*."

Rachael emptied the cup into Jacob. "That's enough for now. Can you tell me what happened?"

Jacob stared at the ceiling.

"Bigun and me, we was gawn head for Boonsboro until all this stuff settled down. 'Tween us eatin' them biscuits you made us an' our comin' up on the Hog Trough Road, well, life sorta took some unexpected turns, I reckon."

"Unexpected? You mean this battle?" asked Rachael.

"Yep. Left the house late last night, headed for Hog Trough, an' we decided to look in on all the commotion up by the church. Dadgum stupid-ass thing to do!"

"You wanted that rifle real bad, didn't you?" Rachael asked, shaking her head.

"I reckon I did," Jacob said, his voice fading in reflection. "We decided to take a little nap in one of Reel's fields until mornin'. Didn't figure on the battle crankin' up so soon. Artillery woke us before the sun had a chance, an' we scrambled.

"Weren't long before we come across the Rebel army, a whole tangle of 'em around the church. Bodies everywhere, Rebel an' Yank. Rebs were hollerin and carryin on like they just whipped the whole Yankee army. I seen bluecoats runnin up the Hagerstown Pike and the Smoketown Road and through Miller's fields. Looked sure 'nough like a whippin'.

"Rebs were laughin and smackin us in the back like we were kinfolk and shoutin after them Yanks, 'Run, you blue devils!' Bigun an me just watched. It was a sight!

"Some reb sent me in the direction of a stack of captured rifles by the church."

"Dunkard Church? Imagine that," Rachael said, observing the irony.

"Yeah. I seen me a rifle layin on top of a dead Yankee, so I picked it up. Hell, I always wanted me one, an' this-un was free."

"Why a dead Yankee?"

"I don't know. I reckon 'cause it'd been battle-tested. I don't know, Rachael. It was a *Yankee* Springfield! Weren't doin' him much good anymore."

"Then what?"

"Bigun grabbed him a rifle, too. A soldier walked up to us an' strung cartridge boxes around our necks an' told us to come on. Still got my five dollar gold, I think. Wait, where's my shirt? It was in my shirt pocket."

Rachael reached into Jacob's pants pocket and pulled out the coin. A bullet-sized dent cupped the coin. Rachael showed the coin to Jacob.

Jacob examined it. "That explains the hard blow I felt right after ... This coin probably saved my life."

"Right after? Right after what, Jacob?"

"Me an' Bigun started down the Hagerstown Pike, holdin these rifles, me feelin' like a Rebel soldier. We got to Hog Trough and saw more Rebs than I ever seen in one place. They'd torn down the fences and stacked the rails in front of 'em. This was no family reunion, Rachael. They'd made a battle line out of our road, Rachael, *our road*.

"A sergeant persuaded us into line, and before we could explain we weren't no soldiers, we found ourselves lookin out across Roulette's fields. Men–boys mostly– squeezed into that road like pumpkins in a harvest wagon, waitin on the Yankees to come, rifles restin on fence rails like crocodiles in the sun. And come they did, blue hornets at a *stingin festival*. Bull said the elephant was comin'. *Damn*, was he right!"

Jacob fingered the bent gold.

"Bull? Elephant? Jacob—"

"Before long, the whole world blew up. Somebody gave the order to fire, and the whole world just *blew up*, ten thousand madmen in a free-for-all firefight, bullets whizzin' like hell turned inside out. Me and Bigun was shootin at Yankees like I don't know what, just tryin to stay alive, shoot or get shot. They kept comin and droppin and comin and droppin. *Our road*, Rachael, and Roulette's and Piper's fields, in an instant changed into fertile ground for the devil's garden.

"Weren't long until the boys on the line were gettin shot, too, fence rails be damned. I never figured a man able to withstand such as I seen, Rachael. But, then, I didn't just *see* it, I was *in* it. Soldiers throwin down muskets too hot an' clogged to fire, takin' up flags from fallen friends, shakin their fists, darin' death.

"I seen a flag-holder hit with six or seven bullets, one right after another, and he still managed to fling 'em the finger before they knocked him down.

"I seen a Yankee standin' on a boulder out in Roulette's field, plain as balls on a bull, firin' down on rebs and shoutin' at his own men to join him on that rock. Far as I know, no Reb touched him. Honor of battle, I reckon.

"There was a fella from North Carolina that saved my life, twice! I forget his name but not what he did. He took a saber through the body after shootin down a man about to shoot me. Then he killed the man with the saber. Damnedest thing I ever seen, and it happened like a flash of lightning!"

"Nobody had no time to think or nothin. All the screamin and shoutin and explosions and curses, men laughin like it was a great big joke, an Irish wedding, an' boys, God, those *poor* boys, beggin for their mamas or wives or girlfriends before they took their last breath. And the *blood*, Rachael, the *blood*— "

"Shhhh! Jacob, Jacob, rest, my sweet. You must rest now," Rachael urged, her hand touching his lips.

Rachael took a breath. Two days ago, Jacob and Roswell argued about the merits of this war, about committing to one cause over the other, about fighting. It seemed to Rachael she had hardly had time enough to pee before one friend was dead and the other recovering from the battle.

"More water, please?"

"Just a bit. Take slow sips. There."

"Thanks. All my jabberjawin' has worn me out."

"Jacob, there's somethin you've got to know."

"What?"

"You're not going to believe who I saw at Killing's Cave last evening."

Rachael dabbed Jacob's mouth.

"Who?"

"Jacob, if you killed Claggett at the bridge yesterday, then we've had the first resurrection since Jesus Christ."

"What in the name of Judas are you talkin' about?"

"I'm talkin' about I saw Claggett at the cave!"

"What? That cain't *be,* Rachael. I *killed* that son of a bitch, put a bullet through his chest!"

"Calm down, Jacob. I hear what you're saying, but hear me, too. He was there at the cave, I *saw* him, and now he's got Jesse and the children. Took 'em away to God knows where. Some old man handed me this note. Here, read it."

Jacob sipped more water and read the paper.

"My God. Rachael, Bigun is outside doing a favor for me. Send him up here as soon as you see him."

Rachael heard groans, turned, and saw the groggy Union sergeant coming out of his induced sleep.

"Forward, double-quick! For God's sake, men, come on! *Faugh-a-Ballagh!"*

Moment of Truth

Rachael pushed the man gently to the pallet and pillow as he tried to rise.

"Shhh! You're hurt badly, sir. You must lie still." She turned facing the door. "I need some opium here!"

Blood soaked the stump's dressing. Rachael peeled away the gooey linens and hastily wrapped fresh cloth around the stump.

"God, it hurts!" the sergeant mumbled, trying to raise his head. "Please, lift my leg so that my knee is bent. Where am I hit?"

Rachael bent the sergeant's right leg.

"The other leg."

Rachael paused. "I cannot, sir," she confessed.

"Why–*ouch!*–why not, for the love of Pete? Where am I hit?"

"Your left leg, sir. And your right hand."

The sergeant traced his left hand down his leg. Afraid of what he might encounter but resolved to know the truth, he inched his fingers toward the knee. He felt warm wetness. He caressed the area and lifted his hand.

"Oh, my God, Jesus!" he shouted, staring at the crimson upon his fingers. He looked into Rachael's tear-filled green eyes.

Stillness descended upon Sergeant Brooks as he gazed into Rachael's eyes. He lowered his hand and raked the blood from his fingers onto the floor. He brushed aside Rachael's hair tickling his neck and smiled.

"Where'd they find a flower like you," he said with the calm of a June breeze. "God has been good to me this day."

The sergeant raised his fingers, took the tears from her cheek, and smeared them on his face.

"Angels weep for the dead," he whispered.

Rachael smiled.

Chapter 18

Unnoticed amid the hodge-podge of green trees and the tangle of underbrush, Bigun trotted with the folded Confederate colors toward the sycamore, as instructed by Jacob. He stepped over bramble and rocks, his sturdy hand firm over the concealed battle flag. The mid-afternoon sun pressed its heat against his back. Bigun stopped to wipe drops of sweat from his eye. He listened. The fight had taken a discernable shift southeastward of Sharpsburg. Limping wounded and deserters passed, heads down, ignoring Bigun.

Reaching the tree, Bigun pulled the banner from his shirt and tucked it inside a hole large enough to stuff an artillery tube.

"Whatchu doin there, nigger?" shouted a Confederate soldier.

Startled, Bigun stood, his back toward the soldier. "Why, I's–I's just makin water, suh."

"On yer *knees*, boy?"

"I gots me the pox, suh," Bigun replied, turning around. "Hard to piss anymo' lessen I gits low," Bigun lied, hoping the Rebel's ignorance of diseases matched his disheveled, shriveled appearance.

"I seen somethin red down yonder, boy. Whatchu up to, anyway?" the soldier asked with suspicion, craning his neck.

"Nothin, sir. Jus makin water's all."

"Where you b'long? You somebody's?" the soldier pried.

"Yessuh, down yonduh," Bigun said, pointing to the Hoffman house.

"Why ainchu down there?"

"I has been, suh, helping wit de wounded an' such. Jus took me a piss break. I be goin right back directly." Bigun remained steadfast, but his anxiety quickened.

"You ain't runnin, are you, boy?"

"*Runnin?* Why, *hell no*, suh," Bigun replied, shaking his head and shifting his weight from foot to foot. "What I mean is, why would I wawna go an' do a thang like dat, what wit de whole Rebel army right on top of me … suh?"

"Jus the same, I reckon I'll come take me a look at whatchu got back there, boy," the soldier said as he stepped from the dust of the Landing Road into the stubble.

Bigun closed his fist around a knife in his belt and stiffened.

"Johnson! Whatchu doin down there, Johnson? Git your stinkin ass up here!" shouted another soldier at the Hoffman house. Johnson turned and trotted to the command.

Bigun released a sigh and watched as the soldier melted into the confusion and commotion of the living and the half-dead. He set the opening of the tree, facing oblique away from the road, with a cover of branches and bushes and began his walk back to Hoffman's. He glanced back a time or two, making sure the site was not conspicuous.

Returning to Jacob's house-turned-hospital, Bigun slowed his gait and stared with awe at a sight bathed in the surreal of hell. Soldiers, red with blood, black with powder, and drenched with sweat, writhed on the ground like maggots in a dead possum.

Surgeons' aides skipped over the seething landscape, careful to avoid tramping the living. The air reeked with the pungency of death, overpowering the woodsy odor of browning leaves; the sweet scent of ripened corn; and the dry, earthy smell of hay. Men, no longer soldiers, issued their final utterances.

"Water!"

Bigun stopped at the well. He dipped the ladle into the bucket and stooped at the head of man shot through both kidneys and the shoulder. The wounded man feebly reached for the blur of motion he could barely discern. Bigun tilted the ladle at the man's lips, spilling a few drops on the man's chin and neck.

"Boy!" shouted an aide. "That water's for the livin!"

"But, suh, dis man, he's–"

"That man's as good as dead. This water is for those with a chance. If you want to help, get inside and strip some bandages!"

"Yassuh, but–"

"Now!"

The wounded soldier's dying eyes watched as Bigun poured the water back into the bucket.

"Wa-water. Please!"

Bigun paused. There was no enmity, no color line, no philosophical barriers in this man's eyes. Bigun reached again for the ladle and placed it at the man's opened, cotton-dry mouth. He poured in a few drops before an aide kicked the ladle from his hands. Water splashed on the dying man's face, a brief, blissful shower.

"I said *now*, nigger."

Bigun glared, stood, at once eager to hear the sound of the aide's neck snapping in his hands. Saying nothing,

Bigun walked toward the house. He glanced back and pondered the misery of the wounded, the foolhardy arbitration of deciders, and the nonsense of a world out of its mind. Neither national affiliation nor color of skin mattered to Bigun at this moment of abject human vulnerability. He saw only the savagery of war, the suffering of flesh, the stupidity of humanity. These were not the ways of God! He wondered what God's ways were. Patience, perhaps. Perseverance. Steadfastness. He thought about the centuries-old plight of generations of slaves, about himself, and about his family. So much to think about. Too much.

Bigun waded past the ugliness and haste of field surgery and surged up the stairs in search of Jacob.

"Bigun!"

"Miss Rachael, thank God Almighty you is awright! Hep you wit dem bandages, ma'am?"

"No thanks. Bigun, Jacob's here, upstairs in his room. He's hurt bad, I'm afraid."

"Yes'm. I know. I brung 'im here."

"You–you brought Jacob here? But how?"

"I's wit 'im, ma'am, when he got shot. We was together, down at Hog Trough. Did he tell you 'bout it?"

"He did; said y'all were fightin with the Rebels."

"Weren't 'cause we wanted to, ma'am. We found ourse'ves in a situation. Shoot or get shot, I reckon. It was a damned sight, ma'am, pardon my language."

"Yes," Rachael agreed, staring out the window. "I can see how it must have been … a damned sight. You okay?"

"I's fine, ma'am. You know about Jesse and the chillun?"

"They're doing fine, Bigun," Rachael lied. "I'll tell you about it later."

"Tell me 'bout what later, Missy?"

Rachael ignored the question.

"Can I talk wit Jacob?" Bigun asked.

Rachael thought for a moment.

"Go ahead. There's something very important he needs to tell you, show you. Don't know if he's awake. Don't take too long, now. There's a Yankee soldier up with him, lost his leg and hand. Don't reckon he'll make it."

"Yes'm. Thank you, ma'am."

Bigun entered Jacob's room, the smell of chloroform and bandages and blood smacking him. He saw Jacob, eyes closed.

"J-Jacob?" he whispered. "Jacob, is you awake?"

Jacob stirred. "Bigun? Bigun!"

"I's here, boss. Done whachu tol' me wit de flag. How you feelin?"

"I've had better days," Jacob said, coughing. "Sycamore tree?"

"Yassuh."

"Problems?"

"Nawsuh, none to speak of. Had a soldier ax me what I's up to, but he didn't see nothin. How de Yankee?"

"'Preciate it. Yankee? What Yankee?"

"On de flo, I spose. Rachael said he–"

"Let me see him."

"Jacob, you ain't in no condition–"

"Let me *see* him!" Jacob insisted, struggling to prop his body on his elbows. Bigun assisted.

Jacob stared at the soldier in blue. Images of the Hog Trough Road fight raced through his mind as if someone had spilled a boxful of daguerreotypes. Before today, he had never seen a man missing half his extremities. Now such a man lay sprawled in his own bedroom. Before today, Jacob Hoffman had not seen much at all.

"Handsome cuss, ain't he?" Jacob thought aloud.

"Reckon who he is, where he's from?" Jacob asked.

At that moment, Brooks stirred. He opened his eyes.

"Rachael?" he called.

"She ain't here," Jacob answered.

"Who-who said that?"

"Over here, on the bed."

"My leg hurts like Satan's butt boil! Havin a hard time of it movin to look your way," Brooks said. "They gave us the devil out there, they did, but I reckon we returned the favor. What unit you with?" he asked.

"Unit? Hell, I'm a unit all my own," Jacob answered, laughing.

"Soldier, what's your unit?" Bigun demanded.

"Hey, Yank, don't get all riled with me. I ain't part of your army. I reckon you'll tell me your name?"

"Benjamin Franklin Brooks, sergeant, 69th New York, Meagher's brigade, Second Corps. Isn't this–isn't this a Union field hospital?"

"Union field hospital, my *ass!* This is my *house*, a *Confederate* field hospital," Jacob answered, pride lacing his voice.

"Dear God!" Brooks said, staring at the ceiling. "Am I a–a prisoner?"

"Well, now, I ain't no expert on the protocol of war, but seems to me anybody who's had his leg and hand shot off ain't a prisoner of nobody's, 'cept himself," Jacob replied. "I reckon they'll let you walk outa here, once you figure out how to use them crutches."

Brooks lifted his handless right arm.

"Jacob! Get back down on that bed this instant!" Rachael shouted as she entered the room.

"Me an' Sergeant Benjamin was havin a talk, Rachael. War an' stuff."

Benjamin Brooks, Rachael thought. *I wonder what the 'F' stands for?*

Rachael inspected Jacob's bandages and gave him a flask of water. The bleeding had stopped. She turned her attention to Brooks.

"I like that cross hanging from your neck," Brooks observed, as Rachael bent over to check his bandages.

Rachael felt a blush. "Thank you … Benjamin." She smiled. "It's an heirloom, my great-great Grandma's."

"Suits you well, embedded in that flower matte."

"Have some water," Rachael whispered.

Brooks drank.

"It smells like–like gardenia," Brooks said.

"This cross? A concoction of my mother's. She's always mixing things together, "fixin nature," she calls it, like they were meant to be together all along, like nature forgot something. I don't rightly know how she does it."

"Rachael," Jacob asked, "may I have more water, please?"

Rachael sighed at the interruption.

"Yes."

Rachael returned with a ladle of water, spilling a few drops on Jacob's head.

"Watch it! Rachael, that's a *Yankee* you're bein all friendly with down there," Jacob muttered gruffly. "Don't forget it was *them* who killed Roswell."

"Jacob Hoffman, since when did you care about sides? You wouldn't be here if not for your selfish desire for–what was it you called it, 'natural things of a man'. He's not a Yankee now; he's a human being. And I'm not bein *all friendly*. They told me to just be nice, to comfort them. I'm *bein nice*, that's all!"

Jacob bristled.

"Gardenia, my *foot!* Jasmine's what it is."

"Let me check your bandages, Jacob. Looks to me like you're going to heal up right nicely. Wound's clean, a bit of pus. Good sign. You always did like my jasmine, didn't you? Have you talked to Bigun?"

"'Bout what?

"The note, remember?"

"Damn, I forgot! Bigun, get over here!"

"Right here, Jacob," he answered.

"Bigun, I got somethin' to say that you ain't gawn believe." Jacob paused.

"Well?"

"Well, seems Claggett, he ain't dead."

"Ain't *dead*? I seen you shoot him in de chest. He fell like a poke of hoss shoes, bleedin like a pig at killin' time. I reckon he 'bout as dead as dey git, boss," Bigun said through an uneasy smile.

"Not accordin to Rachael, he ain't. Said she seen 'im down at the cave last night. It gets worse, Bigun. Claggett's taken Jesse and the kids-"

"Whachu say?"

"-and he wants to exchange them for you."

Bigun stood in stunned silence. "Then who dat you kilt at de creek?"

"I don't know, Bigun. Must've been someone who looked like Claggett an' let us believe that's who it was. Hell, it don't matter. What matters is gettin Jesse and the kids back, without Claggett gettin holt of you."

"How we gawn do dat?"

"Claggett's note told us to meet him down by Rohrbach's Bridge at noon on the 24th."

"I'll meet 'im all right," Bigun said, caressing the blade edge of a Bowie knife, "an' den I'll shove dis knife in his belly an' carve 'im like a trout."

"No weapons, Bigun. Claggett said he'd kill *everybody* if he even suspects any of us got weapons. I don't think it's wise to challenge him on this one."

"You gots a plan?"

"Not yet, but we got a week to figure one out."

"Rachael," Brooks called.

"Right here, Benjamin," Rachael replied.

Benjamin? Jacob thought, eyebrows lifted at Rachael's snug familiarity with Brooks.

"Hurts like hell."

Rachael took Brooks's hand into hers and dabbed his forehead with a damp cloth. Brooks closed his eyes and took a long sniff. The scent of gardenia from Rachael's cross caressed his dreams, and he smiled. Rachael noticed his full lower lip and unblemished teeth. The raven hair and sapphire eyes reached inside and squeezed her spirit. Despite his physical losses, this was a man in full, a man after Rachael's heart. Her attraction swelled.

Chapter 19

Two mornings after the great battle, the sky dawned crisp for the end of summer. Lee's ravaged army had waited for the expected commencement of day two of the fight, like a punch-drunk brawler refusing to go down. The end of the Army of Northern Virginia, even the Confederacy, was McClellan's for the taking. But he would have to *take* it, and the equally pummeled Yankees, suffering their own morning-after hangover, were in no mood to engage Lee's unknown quantity. Lee limped across the Potomac.

The roads on the outskirts of Sharpsburg were sparsely dotted with the curious. Refugees began the slow trickle back to devastated homes and land. Souvenir hunters tramped the fields of no-man's-land, rifling through the pants pockets of the dead, all of which were rebels ignored by Yankee gravediggers, and scavenging anything of value. Voices of unimagined agony, each a Lazarus, begged anything on two legs for a drop of water.

As the day aged, thousands of wounded filled every space in every building, hut, shack, barn and tent for miles around. The air smelled of putrid flesh, human and animal excrement, and the burn of thousands of pounds of black powder.

A carbon haze hovered over the ground, like specters surprised by their bodies' sudden demise. Trees lay splintered and toppled. Trampled cornstalks rested beside harvests of the dead. Open fields once lush with the green of grass and the rainbow of wildflowers now languished in the debris of war. Loved ones and burial details trod careful paths among the deceased as they grappled with the enormity of where to begin.

Rachael, armed with fresh bandages, came into Jacob's bedroom to tend the wounds. Jacob had an advantage. Though shot through the body, he lay in his own bed in his own home on his own land. He slept. Brooks lay in a deepening pain, the quickness of his amputations beginning to tell.

Rachael glanced over at Jacob. Then, she turned her attentions to Brooks. Her heart jumped.

"Rachael, so good–*God, my God!*–so good to see you," Brooks said with a tired voice, bolts of pain slicing through his leg. "Let me smell your jasmine."

"It's gardenia, Benjamin," she replied. "Just for you."

Brooks smiled, eyes wincing. "I thought Jacob said–"

"Shhh. Never mind what Jacob said."

Rachael bent over Brooks. She took a quick glance at his wrist and then his leg. She was struck by the rancid odor of rotting flesh, her head taking an abrupt, instinctive snap away. She carefully unwrapped the dressing from his leg.

"It ain't good, is it?" he asked.

Rachael paused.

"Now don't you worry about anything. It's got the pus. Doc says look for the pus. That means it's healing."

After administering some morphine and redressing the stump, Rachael dampened a cloth and wiped Brooks' forehead. As she patted his cheek with the cloth, Brooks opened his eyes and curled his fingers around her wrist.

Rachael looked at Brooks, the blue of his eyes penetrating her soul like the words of Emily Dickinson. At once, she wanted to kiss him, a sentiment shared by Brooks. He took his right arm and nudged Rachael's neck forward. She offered no resistance. As they kissed, surrounded by Jacob's house, his room, even him, she surrendered all thoughts of Jacob Hoffman.

Jacob stirred, shaking Rachael from her bliss.

"Rest, Benjamin. I'll be right here."

Rachael walked over to Jacob.

"Good morning, Jacob," she said with a songful lilt.

"Where? Who? Oh. Rachael, it's you."

"Have some water, Jacob. I'll go scramble you some eggs and–"

"No, Rachael, nothin' now. Ain't up to eatin' right yet."

"But you need your strength, Jacob. I'll just–"

"Rachael, please! I ain't hungry now. Just the water."

Rachael checked Jacob's wound and changed his bandage.

"Looks good, Jacob," she said.

"Good? How can a hole through my body possibly look good?" he asked, irritated that Rachael might be so dismissive of his plight.

"What I meant was, it's looking better, healing up. I don't see any signs of infection or–"

"Rachael, you wouldn't know infection if it was a coiled rattler.

"Jacob I know what to look for; doc told me. Now you rest while I go make some breakfast."

"I told you, I don't want nothin'," Jacob insisted.

"Fine. Others do. I'll be back shortly. Anything you need before I go?"

"Bedpan."

Rachael retrieved the bedpan and waited for Jacob.

"I see you got your easel set up over yonder," Jacob said, looking at the window.

"Why–why yes. Yes, I have," Rachael answered.

"Whatchu paintin' today? Another sunset? I reckon there ain't much of a landscape left to paint anymore."

"Oh, nothing, really. Just dabbing on some colors to see what pops up," she said, smiling.

"I know that smile," Jacob observed. "That's your smile of mischief."

"Why, Jacob Hoffman, I am not a woman of mischief–"

"*Not* a woman of mischief? That's like sayin' Lincoln's not a man of politics. Hell, you *invented* mischief!" Jacob said, laughing.

Jacob Hoffman, I won't stand here and listen to your whining. I'm going to make breakfast."

"I'm not whining. Let me see your painting."

"It's not–it's not finished. I'll show you when it's finished, not before."

Rachael took the bedpan and emptied it.

"You look especially beautiful today, Rachael," Jacob offered with a conciliatory tone.

"Why, thank you, Jacob."

"How's it look outside?" Jacob asked.

"Well, we have wounded scattered all over the yard waiting on somebody to treat them. There's just so many of them. About all we can do now is give water and tend to the ones who might survive. It's the Godawfulest thing I ever saw, Jacob. Those poor men!"

Jacob stared at the ceiling. "Our road's a mess, Rachael."

"Our road?"

Moment of Truth

"Hog Trough. *That* was the Godawfulest thing I ever saw."

"Rest now," Rachael urged.

Rachael passed by Brooks on her way out of the room. He followed her every step, a thankful smile upon his face. She glanced at him but did not turn her head. Each knew the other's thoughts.

Chapter 20

The morning of September 20 found McClellan's Army of the Potomac in complete occupation of the killing fields of Sharpsburg. Lee's pummeled Army of Northern Virginia had retreated across the Potomac River into Shepherdstown and beyond. Though not the overwhelming battlefield victory Lincoln had hoped for, Lee's abandonment of Sharpsburg was close enough. Because of this weeping of blood and gnashing of flesh, the following days would alter the course of the war, the opinions of the world, and the future of two nations.

Opportunities to destroy Lee's army, and end the war then and there, lay silenced among the dead and desolate of the field. History would speak of them often. Hooker's First Corps flop in the Cornfield; Sedgwick's disaster in the woods around the Dunkard Church; failure of Sumner's Second Corps to press the breach at Hog Trough Road; and Burnside's delayed, piecemeal assault on a bridge bottleneck and subsequent repulse by A.P. Hill on the Confederate right flank. Each of these failures spelled another two and a half years of bloodshed.

The great and terrible day of September 17, a horrific slinging of lead, iron, and blood on scales heretofore unmatched and unimaginable, produced in the days following a vacuous, resonant silence, like a pulling tide before a tsunami, replaced with the sickening, pathetic cries of thousands of wounded.

Lee's army stayed on the fields of Sharpsburg the day after the battle, either in utter defiance or from sheer exhaustion, perhaps both. The gamble paid off, allowing Lee time to gain the strength to retreat across the Potomac. McClellan, still convinced of Lee's numerical superiority, waited and retrieved his wounded.

Among the more fortunate of the wounded lay Benjamin Franklin Brooks and Jacob Hoffman. These were among the first evacuated to field hospitals, before overcrowding became an issue of desperate importance.

The healing of Jacob's wound progressed more rapidly than expected, due likely to the bullet's clean passage through his body. Brooks's wound, conversely, took a turn for the worse. The area around his amputated left leg blackened, and the pain became intolerable and unmanageable.

"Doctor, it's Sergeant Brook's leg, sir," an aide reported. "Necrosis."

Doctors, whom never before had seen a bullet wound, found themselves saturated with the blood from thousands of bullet and shell fragment wounds. Now came the aftermath of the necessity of their haste to treat the volume of wounds. Gangrene.

Rachael kneeled draped over Brooks, touching a soaked sponge to his lips and whispering words of comfort in his ear.

"Take it off," begged Brooks, "please, take it off."

"Doctor's on his way. Shhh!" Rachael said. "Here, smell this."

She pulled the gardenia cross from around her neck and placed it in Brooks's palm, wrapping his fingers around it. She lifted his hand to his nose. The sweetness of the gardenia cut through his agony and removed from his mind, if only for a moment, any doubt of his survival.

"Step aside, please," the surgeon demanded.

Rachael complied.

Meanwhile, Jacob managed to lift his healing body from his bed. He needed a bedpan, and no one had heard his requests for one. Rachael gave her complete attention to the surgeon and to Brooks, a fact that did not escape Jacob's notice.

Jacob wobbled. He grabbed the bedpost and maintained his balance, and in doing so noticed Rachael's easel near the far window. Stepping over to view her painting, he was aghast by what he found.

Thinking the painting was of himself, perhaps of both him and Brooks recuperating, or maybe a restless brushing of the oak outside his window, instead he found Rachael had painted herself strolling along the sunset-bathed Hog Trough Road holding the arm of a Yankee soldier, of Benjamin Franklin Brooks.

He looked at Rachael, mindless of his discovery. The cross from her neck was gone, as were the jasmine flowers from her hair. The unmistakable fragrance of gardenia filled the air.

"We're going to put you to sleep, now, soldier," the doctor said.

"Do good, doc," Brooks said.

"Ditto for me, doctor," Rachael said. She leaned down and whispered something into Brooks's ear. Both smiled.

"Rachael, water!" Jacob lied.

Annoyed, Rachael sighed. "Coming, Jacob."

Rachael brought a cupful of water to Jacob.

"You seem to be doing much better, Jacob. I'm so happy. Now you can–"

"You love him, don't you?"

"W–what?"

"You're in love with Brooks, aintchu?"

"Jacob, what are you talking–"

"I saw the painting, Rachael," Jacob said, irritated by her look of innocent surprise. "After all this, you're still a dreamer. The man can't walk, Rachael!"

Rachael glanced over at the easel. "Oh, Jacob."

"It's okay, Rachael. Really, it is."

"Jacob, I never meant–"

"Don't ... Rachael. Don't explain. Explanations just turn into lies. I love you, Rachael. No lie." Jacob took a breath and stared at the ceiling. He issued a soft chuckle, as if he realized for the first time the obvious answer to a great riddle. "I said it. That wasn't so hard."

Rachael's eyes welled. A tear cut a trail down her cheek, slowly, like a raindrop on a windowpane. It was the first she had heard Jacob utter those words.

"Bedpan, please?" Jacob asked.

Chapter 21

"I got me an idea, Bigun," Jacob said, breaking what seemed an interminable silence.

It was Wednesday morning, September 24, two hours before the appointed time to meet Claggett at the Rohrbach Bridge for the exchange.

Jacob, Isaac, and Bigun had sat at the bloodstained kitchen table since supper the night before, discussing ways to get Jesse and the children safely back from Claggett. Ideas were discarded as soon as they breathed life.

"I hope it's a good-un, boss."

"Won't know 'til we try it, but let me tell you."

"Why don't we just hide somebody behind the trees above the bridge and shoot the bastard?" Isaac asked, irritated that a solution so simple had not already been thought of.

"Cain't do that, Daddy," Jacob answered. "I reckon Claggett's done thought about that and will have one or more of Bigun's family strapped right up against him, like a second set of clothes. Cain't risk shootin' the wrong one. What if we miss? Besides, he'll be watchin' every approach."

"No, I suppose there *is* that risk. So, what's your plan, son?"

"Daddy, I figure we can get one of 'em free right off, just by bluffin' him into thinkin' Bigun won't budge until one of 'em *is* freed. It's a risk, too, I know, but hear me out.

"When me an' Bigun were down in the Hog Trough in the middle of the fight, there wasn't a lot of time to think about much, except rammin' a bullet down the barrel an' pullin' the trigger. I mean, I cain't be sure I ever actually shot a man, but I know I kept 'em thinkin' about it.

"Anyway, thinkin' back on all that, I remember how the mere sight of a regiment's colors got the blood up more'n just 'bout anything. Men would stop whatever it was they were doin' or shootin' at and kill the man holdin' the flag. 'Kill the flag man!' they'd shout."

"Son, I don't want to hear you talking about that battle or this war anymore," Isaac demanded.

Jacob stared at Isaac. "Ain't nothin' you can say to me about that," Jacob said, rejecting his Father's demands. "I'm my own man, now, Daddy, whether you like that or not. I've seen an' done things you won't never see an' do as long as you draw a breath, an' I figure I earned my independence. Bigun, too."

"Keep talkin'," Bigun said.

Isaac shut his mouth, an inferno of anger seething inside. Freedom was one thing. Independence was another.

"Daddy, I got me more than a bullet at the Hog Trough. I got me a flag, too, a Rebel flag."

Isaac's eyes flew open; his jaw dropped.

"Jesus of Nazareth, Jacob! How in the name of Horatio Sharpe did you come by another cursed rebel flag, of all things?"

"Well, there's been a few of 'em around here lately," Jacob said, reminding Isaac of the obvious. "About all I can say to you, Daddy, is that you had to be there. You'll never understand what I saw, what I experienced.

But I'll say this, too. Many a brave man fell defendin' that very flag. Same with the Union boys an' the Stars and Stripes. I seen at least two Yankees swing their rifle barrels away from at me and aim instead at an unarmed flag-bearer. That Rebel flag saved my ass, Daddy. I got that very flag hid, an' we're going to use it to get Bigun's people back. Ironic, ain't it?"

"How we gawn do dat, boss?" Bigun asked.

"As soon as we get one of the children back–which means you're going to have to be mighty convincin', Bigun–I'm going to unfurl that reb flag, bigger'n a hoop skirt at a barn dance. It's the next to last thing Claggett will expect to see."

"What's the *last* thing he'll expect to see?" Isaac said, filled with stubborn doubt.

"A bullet comin' straight at his face," Jacob answered.

"A *bullet*! And just *who* is going to pull the trigger?"

"You are, Daddy," Jacob replied, smiling.

"Have you lost your mind, young man?"

"That big, bloodied, battle-torn flag will shine in Claggett's eyes like the afternoon sun. As soon as he notices it, his guard will drop. That's when you shoot 'im, Daddy."

"And what if I miss?"

"At five feet? Not even a Dunkard Baptist misses at five feet."

"It's a goot plan, suh," Bigun agreed.

"How so, may I ask?" Isaac argued.

"Because, Daddy, you are the *last* person on earth Claggett would expect to be armed, much less shoot a man. He's going to check me an' Bigun for weapons, *that* you can count on. But it won't even occur to him to check you, a devout Dunkard Baptist."

"With what pistol?" Bigun asked.

Moment of Truth

"The pocket Colt my granddaddy gave me. It's small enough to fit under your belt, above your butt. You gotta be quick about it. No slips, no mistakes, no second thoughts. It's 11:00. Bigun, you get the flag. Let's go."

Upstairs, Rachael nursed Brooks's twice-amputated leg. No recurrence of gangrene. Two voices laughed. Jacob heard. He glanced at the kitchen ceiling. How strange it felt, the love of his life rejecting him for a one-legged Yankee. How awkward he felt, Rachael and Brooks upstairs in *his* bedroom.

Brooks survived the Hog Trough fight, same as Jacob. Perhaps Brooks fired the bullet that passed through Jacob. Perhaps Jacob's bullets were among the hundreds that Brooks heard zipping past. Now Brooks passed through Jacob.

Rachael was Brooks's flag. *Life had taken some odd turns the past week*, Jacob thought.

Jacob walked up the stairs to his bedroom, making sure his steps were loud enough to announce the approach of another person.

"Excuse me, please," Jacob said, peeking into the room, his room. "We're going to get Bigun's family back. I need to get my Colt."

Jacob retrieved the mahogany trinket box in which was stashed the pistol. Lifting the gun, he stopped. His eyes stared hard at the dried jasmine, marking moments of a purer, innocent past. He smiled, despite knowing she was no longer his, not sure if the fragrance he smelled was real or imagined.

"Can't take the memories," he whispered.

"What'd you say, Jacob?" Rachael asked, rubbing Brooks's hand.

"What? Oh, nothing. We'll be back in a while. Wish us luck. We're going to need it."

"Jacob," Brooks called out.

Jacob turned and stopped.

"You're a fine man, Jacob, as honorable a man as I've ever known. God be with you."

Jacob gave a slight nod.

"Rachael, may I have a word with you, alone?" Jacob asked.

Seeking approval, Rachael turned to Brooks.

"Go ahead, Rachael," he said with a nod.

Rachael patted Brooks's hand. "I'll be right back," she whispered.

Rachael and Jacob walked downstairs.

"What is it, Jacob?"

"Us, Rachael. What happened? How did we lose it?"

"I don't know, Jacob," Rachael answered, sighing. "Maybe we never had it to lose. It took a war to bring this country to its senses. Us, too, I reckon."

"Yeah." Jacob paused, reflective. "Dragonflies," he said.

"Dragonflies?"

"Devil's darnin' needles. Suck your brains right out, make a mind forget everything," Jacob said, smiling. His smile dropped. "Hearts never forget."

Rachael returned the smile and lowered her head. She reached up and gave Jacob a kiss on the jaw, for old-time's sake.

"Took a ride with my Grandmother yesterday," Rachael said. "She needed the sun. We got to Hog Trough Road. I told her what had happened here, what had happened to you. She looked around and noticed the rust-red tint of the ground. Maybe it was the sun, but the ground looked reddish. The red stretched as far as she was able to walk.

"She stopped, finally, and turned to me and said, 'This ain't Hog Trough no more. It's a bloody lane.' I guess we're a bit like Hog Trough. The blood of change stained us. We're not what we were," she said.

"Always the literate one. You were my Jasmine," Jacob said.

Rachael lowered her head. "Be careful with Claggett, Jacob."

Jacob touched Rachael's hair and turned to join the others outside.

"Let's get this done," he said, handing the Colt to Isaac.

Bigun gave Jacob the folded flag, bold in its red and blue design, emboldened by its paint of blood. He tucked it inside his shirt high up against his back.

"Six shots, Daddy. You might only get one."

Isaac took the pistol and shoved it between his belt and pants, just above his butt.

"Leave the talkin' to me," Jacob said.

The three set out. The men said nothing on their way to Rohrbach's Bridge.

"That's far enough!" a voice shouted from the direction of the creek.

Isaac's wagon slowed to a stop on the Lower Bridge Road, roughly twenty yards from the bridge.

"I see you come alone," Claggett said, stepping out from under the bridge to the path paralleling the creek. "Well, well, Isaac Hoffman, good to see *you* once again. Bigun, you're lookin' mighty healthy. Wouldn't want to scrape with you. I do believe a debt is come due."

Jacob and Isaac looked at Bigun, puzzlement in their eyes.

"He hasn't told you fellas? Well, let me fill you in. Three years ago, at Harpers Ferry, Bigun participated as one of John Brown's raiders. I know, because I was there, too, deliverin' a load of nails from the Furnace. To make a long story short, mainly because I ain't got the patience to tell it all, I kept Bigun from the hangman's noose in return for the privilege of his services, beginning, oh, now."

"Where's Jesse and my young-uns?" Bigun demanded with the scowl of a cornered bear.

"They're safe, my friend. Come on out, you three. You see, normally I would have never let them leave my side, but I had to test you for weapons. Had you any weapons, surely you would have tried to kill me with those three out of the line of fire. You didn't. I took a chance, but a calculated one. So, Bigun, if you will–"

"Let Little Jim go first. He goes, I come, or no deal," Bigun said, his voice firm.

"Negotiating, are we? Tell you what, you can have Little Jim. I won't be needin' him. Too scrawny for Charleston summers anyhow. Planters won't give half a penny for a scrawny nigger."

Little Jim looked at his Mama and at Bigun, unsure if the deal had merit.

"Go on, boy!" Claggett shouted with impatience. "Go to your master."

Jacob let out a breath.

"Okay, Bigun, let's go. Charleston's a long way from here."

Just then, Jacob whipped out the Rebel flag, big as a tablecloth, its tattered color flapping in the autumn wind. Claggett dropped his grip on Jesse at the sight of the flag, and gasped in surprise.

In the same moment, Isaac reached behind, yanked out the pocket Colt, thrust it toward Claggett's head, and fired. He missed. The shot, instead, tore into Claggett's throat. Claggett clutched his neck, blood spurting between his madly probing fingers. Bigun took the Colt from Isaac and put the barrel at Claggett's forehead.

"Debt paid," Bigun drawled as he squeezed the trigger and put a finishing bullet into Claggett's skull.

Bigun dropped the revolver and grabbed Jesse.

"Thank you, Jesus!" Jesse shouted.

Chapter 22

The spring of 1863 echoed the angry sounds of combat from the fields of Virginia. Rejuvenated by victories at Fredericksburg at the close of '62 and Chancellorsville in May, Southern high command revisited the objectives, and the promise, of the Maryland Campaign.

By June, Lee's juggernaut again appeared invincible. Lee marched his army north, desperate to take the fight away from an impoverished, torn Virginia and to unhinge the North's war efforts, perhaps convince European powers to ignore Union naval blockades, despite Lincoln's Proclamation of Emancipation. Hopes were high that a Southern victory on Northern ground would compel a war-weary North to sue for peace. Not since Manassas had morale been as supreme.

Jacob stood in the door of Dunkard Church and watched as Southern soldiers marched northward along the Hagerstown Pike, scene of unparalleled combat just eight months earlier. The sight was eerily familiar.

He thought of his childish pursuit of a Springfield rifle and the dead soldier from whom he had acquired it.

He thought about the savagery in the fields before him and the storm within Hog Trough Road, about Sergeant Thomas Rushin, about Bull Stokes and Tucker

McGavin, about his coin, about Bigun, and about the Rebel battle flag.

He thought about the blood, the bones, the bullets flying, the bursting of Pandora's Box on the land of his home, indeed, his very house. He wiped his forehead.

He thought about Roswell, wrapped in the promise of a flag, drawn to his own adventure.

His physical wound suffered in the Bloody Lane had healed, its only evidence a jagged, circular scar. A Yankee for whom he had held no malice shot him down that maniacal September morning.

He thought about the irony of the survival of his flesh and the death of his spirit, his heart. He thought about darning needles and Rachael, about Sergeant Brooks.

Rachael was gone, only the Lord knew where, married to Benjamin Franklin Brooks. For Jacob, this was the wound worse than bullets.

Bigun, Jesse, and their two children had packed their sparse belongings in an Isaac Hoffman-made wagon and journeyed north to Boston. Jacob kept in his pocket a letter written by Bigun, his first, telling of his adventures as a freed man out of the reach of soul drivers. Bigun spoke of joining a black regiment at Camp Meigs, Readville, Massachusetts.

Jacob squinted and peered at the gray cloud obscuring the afternoon sun, its rays blasting out all around the cloud's edges, defying containment. Jacob smiled.

Jacob walked the roads and fields of the Sharpsburg battlefield day after day. His emotional gravity took him each time to Hog Trough Road and to his memories of Rachael. This was their road, Hog Trough. Now it belonged to history, a memorial to the men who fought here, their blood its coronation.

As he stood and gazed along its length, Jacob knew God had a purpose for him. No other explanation satisfied the questions of his deliverance from such a din of violence, of Rachael's deliverance from him.

Jacob kicked pebbles and soldiers' rusted tins and bent to pick up smashed bullets and other debris ignored by souvenir hunters in the battle's wake. The road was calm again, as it had always been before, its fences rebuilt. Jacob wept for the poor souls destroyed that day, futures shot away, the brave men of both armies struck down in a flash of time, a moment of truth.

Near the road's apex, the point where he fought with the Sixth Alabama, Jacob stopped and stared across the fields of corn.

Here, Jacob thought. *I'll bury it here.*

The next day, Jacob rose before the sun. He and Isaac had an order of two wagons to deliver by three o'clock, but there was time. He heated day-old coffee and gulped the steaming liquid as fast as his throat allowed. He looked up the stairs for a moment and sighed.

In his room, Jacob opened the dower chest, swept away cobwebs, and removed the mahogany box. He opened the box and checked its contents one last time.

The box contained the essence of what Jacob was and what he had become.

A few cats' eyes.

A broken antler-handle knife.

A gold coin, dented.

"Buy an adventure," Jacob said with a laugh, a rush of emotion pushing a tear to his eye.

A string-bound fascicle of Emily Dickinson's poems, given to Rachael with a shrug of dissatisfaction by Rachael's cousin.

Jacob held the volume in his palm. "Rachael," he said, "this is the essence of who you were, the spirit I too often ignored."

One of Rachael's paintbrushes, blotched with dried red paint.

"This brush you used to paint your sunset scenes," Jacob observed as he tucked it snug against the box's wall. "And so it was."

Flowers of dried jasmine, three four-leaf clovers, one black-eyed Susan.

"These I'll place inside Miss Emily's book. Poetry should be pretty, you always said. And a bit lucky."

A folded note written by Jacob.

"For history."

Jacob lowered the lid and closed the latch. He brushed both palms across its top, like a coffin. He reached under his mattress and removed the bloodstained, bullet-torn Rebel battle flag he had used to field-dress his wound. With gentle respect, he spread the flag open on his bed and placed the box upside down in the middle. He wrapped the flag around the box, its center star shining center-top of the box.

Jacob gave a deep sigh and turned to go downstairs.

"Where you headed, son?" Isaac asked as he dressed.

"Out," Jacob replied.

"Out? Out where?"

"I'll be back in a while. Biscuits and coffee on the table."

"We got those wagons to deliver," Isaac said. "Don't want to be late."

"We won't. Deliveries are always on time," Jacob replied with a smile.

A long hour later, Jacob set the box on the north embankment of Hog Trough Road, near the apex. He took his shovel and cut the earth two square feet deep. He flung chunks of dirt aside, stopping briefly to wipe the summer sweat. He set down the shovel on the embankment and watched Roulette work the fields through which thousands of Union soldiers had charged and died. He placed the box in the hole, in the middle of the road, and returned the dirt.

Moment of Truth

"Done," he said. "Time to heal."

Jacob Hoffman hoisted the shovel onto his shoulder. He stood erect and gave a salute as he stared down the length of the road.

"To you, fine soldiers of gray and blue. May you bury your past, as I have buried mine."

Jacob turned and began his slow trek home.

No going back now, he thought, as he glanced over his shoulder at the site one last time. *Bloody lane.*

****

Mark parked his car in the lot facing the Bloody Lane. He had spent the morning touring the northern portions of the Sharpsburg battlefield. The day was hot for April and void of the stampede of summer tourists. He grabbed his digital camera and walked toward the intersection of Roulette's Lane and the Bloody Lane.

Mark took scores of photos from an array of angles and formed mental images of what occurred here one hundred forty-four years earlier. As he strolled uphill at the bend in the eroded road, a cooling breeze against his face, he noticed a protrusion from the ground in the middle of the road, like a root with no tree.

Curious, Mark approached the object. This was no root. The object was a square corner, that of a box. He reached down to touch the object. The dry ground held it firm, like concrete. Mark looked around and noticed no other person. He began to scrape the ground away from the object.

After careful excavating, Mark removed the box and pried loose the latch. Lifting the lid, he discovered its remarkable contents. He sifted through each item, stunned with his find. Then he discovered under an embroidered handkerchief a folded piece of paper projecting from a string-bound book of poems.

He laid the paper on the ground and gently lifted
each fold. Inside he found the magnificent swirls and
curves of nineteenth century penmanship. The date, though
faded, read "June 17, 1862." He fingered the antler-handle
knife and read.

"Greetings to you from the bloody lane. For
me, it shall remain Hog Trough Road.
That's a piece of my past I can never bury.

It is three months until the first anniversary
of the great battle at Sharpsburg.

Though you and I shall never meet, I trust
this box and its treasured contents will
reveal to you the person I was and suggest
the person I became.

I am certain history has recorded the events
of September 17, so I will not encumber
your time reciting what you already know.

Instead, I will say this. Rebel and Yankee
fought passionately in these solemn fields of
the Antietam Valley, as they did here in this
road. Each fought for his own reasons, valid
in his own mind. Those killed and wounded
left their reasons in the blood they spilled
here. I fought among them and witnessed
their courage and their struggle. I should
think all Americans are still as brave.

Bravery as I shall never know again was
common among the men who trod these
fields and died among the clover and black-
eyed Susans such that rest within this box.

Moment of Truth

Commitment and dedication were as sweet
as the jasmine.

Battle is anything but poetic, though some
would disagree. Miss Emily wrote, "When
that which is and that which was, apart,
intrinsic, stand; and this brief tragedy of
flesh is shifted like a sand." Sometimes it
takes a poet to reveal battle's truth.

The gold coin bears the impact of a Yankee
bullet. Were it not for this coin in my
pocket in this road, given to me by my
Grandfather two years earlier, you would
not be reading this note, nor thumbing
through the contents of this box. He told me
to buy an adventure. I got my money's
worth.

This box was wrapped in a battle flag of the
Sixth Alabama. Render its remains to
solemn keepsake, and never forget what
these Americans of both armies won and
what they surrendered on 17 September,
1862.

John Jacob Hoffman
Sharpsburg civilian

Mark searched the soil but found no remnant of the
flag. He folded the paper and placed it inside the book of
poems, which he set inside the box. He picked handfuls of
clover and filled the hole, patching the resurrection of a
one-hundred-and-forty-four-year-old wound. He waved his
hand, shooing away a pesky dragonfly, and laid a Black-

eyed Susan on top of the clover. He sat next to the spot and thought.

Just thought.

Cherry blossoms spilled from their branches. He looked up. A great horned owl screeched overhead and swooped among the unseen prey of the fields.